PUFFIN

The Knight a

Terry Jones was born in 1942 in Wales. He read English at Oxford University and retains a passion for medieval history and literature: his study of Chaucer's Knight received wide critical acclaim when it was published some years ago. He became well known to the general public as a member of the Monty Python team. He co-directed *Monty Python and the Holy Grail* and directed *Monty Python's Life of Brian*, *The Meaning of Life* (which won the Grand Jury prize at Cannes in 1983), *Eric the Viking*, *Personal Services* and *The Wind in the Willows* (which won the Best Film in the International Children's Film Festival in Chicago, 1998).

Terry Jones is married and lives in London.

Other books by Terry Jones

THE LADY AND THE SQUIRE

FAIRY TALES
FANTASTIC STORIES
NICOBOBINUS
THE SAGA OF ERIK THE VIKING

TERRY JONES

The
Knight
and the
Squire

Illustrated by
MICHAEL FOREMAN

PUFFIN BOOKS

For Julien

PUFFIN BOOKS

Published by the Penguin Group
Penguin Books Ltd, 80 Strand, London WC2R 0RL, England
Penguin Putnam Inc., 375 Hudson Street, New York, New York 10014, USA
Penguin Books Australia Ltd, Ringwood, Victoria, Australia
Penguin Books Canada Ltd, 10 Alcorn Avenue, Toronto, Ontario, Canada M4V 3B2
Penguin Books India (P) Ltd, 11 Community Centre, Panchsheel Park, New Delhi – 110 017, India
Penguin Books (NZ) Ltd, Cnr Rosedale and Airborne Roads, Albany, Auckland, New Zealand
Penguin Books (South Africa) (Pty) Ltd, 24 Sturdee Avenue, Rosebank 2196 South Africa

Penguin Books Ltd, Registered Offices: 80 Strand, London WC2R 0RL, England

www.penguin.com

First published by Pavilion Books Limited 1997
Published in Puffin Books 1999
6

Text copyright © Fegg Features Ltd, 1997
Illustrations copyright © Michael Foreman, 1999
All rights reserved

The moral right of the author and illustrator has been asserted

Typeset in 11½/14½ Sabon

Made and printed in England by Clays Ltd, St Ives plc

British Library Cataloguing in Publication Data
A CIP catalogue record for this book is available from the British Library

ISBN 0–140–38804–4

· 1 ·

I suppose the things that people did six hundred years ago were just as real to them when they were doing them as the things you and I were doing two minutes ago are to us now.

Certainly the water felt very real on Tom's leg, as he sat dangling one foot in the duck-pond, six hundred years ago, on the morning that this story begins. After making a few ripples, he looked across at the village in which his father had grown up and in which his grandfather had grown up and in which his great grandfather had lived and died, and he suddenly gave a great grin, crossed his eyes, shouted out: 'Saladin!' and toppled slowly forwards into the duck-pond.

The village priest, who happened to be passing by, on his way to sell his dog, hurried over.

'Thomas! Thomas! That was a *pointless* thing to do!' he said as he tried to pull Tom out. But Tom was laughing so much he couldn't stand up.

'There's nothing funny about it! It was a silly, *pointless* thing to do! I saw! You did it deliberately!'

'I did,' agreed Tom, but then he started laughing again, until the priest pulled him out and shook him.

'God did not put us on this earth to waste our lives in

pointless, stupid actions.' But the more he shook him, the more Tom laughed.

'I know,' agreed Tom, 'but . . .'

'Then *why* did you do it?' asked the priest.

'I don't know,' said Tom. But he did. He knew exactly why.

'You've got brains, Thomas, haven't you?' the priest was saying.

'Yes,' said Tom.

'Then use them!'

Tom tried to pull himself together. He bit his lip and concentrated on looking at the priest's ridiculously large feet, as he strode off. Tom tried not to think about the way the water was running down the insides of his own legs and into his new shoes, because he knew that would only make him start laughing again.

'If I can manage not to laugh for as long as that duck stays under water, I'll be all right,' he was telling himself. But just at that moment the priest turned back on him so suddenly that it somehow made Tom choke on another laugh.

The priest looked pained.

'Thomas! Thomas! You are the cleverest by far . . . You could be destined for great things, if only . . .' He looked Tom up and down.

'If only I wasn't such a fool,' Tom thought to himself. 'That's what you're going to say.'

But the priest was hurrying away, with the dog yapping happily after him.

The dog didn't know it was going to be sold. As a matter of fact I could tell you a whole story about that dog, for the most incredible adventures happened to it after it was sold by the priest. But this is not the time or place to go into all those things.

That afternoon, Tom and his sister Kate were lying among the corn stooks, listening to the reapers in the next field as they grunted and sang and the blades swished.

Tom was laughing and so was Kate.

'I *knew* he was looking at me!' said Tom. 'If you could have just seen his face!'

'Did he get his feet wet?' asked Kate.

'A bit,' said Tom.

'But it *was* a stupid thing to do,' grinned Kate.

'That's the whole point,' said Tom.

'Why do you enjoy annoying the priest so much, Tom?'

Tom shrugged and said, 'Uh-oh! Trouble!'

Another voice was cutting across the summer sounds of the meadows.

'Thomas! Thomas! Come quickly!'

Katie gave Tom the good luck sign that the two of them reserved for moments of Mortal Danger and Direst Peril, and Tom sprinted off across the field towards Old Molly Christmas.

'Oh look at you!' the old woman cried, as he appeared through a gap in the hedge. 'The blessed saints preserve us! Tidy your hair! Your new shoes! Straighten your stockings! Quickly now!'

And Old Molly was off across the village green, heading for the tumbledown house where she had cared for the two children since the plague times.

As they rounded a corner, Tom nearly fell off his horse – well he would have done if he'd been riding one. As it was he more or less fell off his legs.

'Who are *they*?' he whispered.

'You'll find out! You'll find out!' Old Molly was muttering crossly as she headed straight towards them.

There were three men apparently waiting for Tom. Two of them wore the red livery of the Abbot of Selby and the third was wrapped in a cloak of crimson and velvet – despite the fact that it was a bright summer's day.

Old Molly pushed Tom forward with a 'Here he is', and Tom took off his cap and stared at the floor. The three men looked at him for some time, while he tried to straighten his hair. Then the man in the cloak said, 'We happened to be passing by,' as if that explained everything.

By this time Katie had turned up, and was standing in the gap in the hedge. Tom didn't see her, but he could feel her presence. He could also feel the presence of a lot of other villagers – Margery Red Cap, Maude the baker's wife and her three children, Dorothy Landless, and Father James and some of the other men too old to help with the harvest – all standing staring from a safe distance.

At this moment the man in the cloak did something rather odd. He suddenly spoke in a language none of the villagers could understand.

Tom looked at the ground and said nothing while the villagers all stared at him. The stranger repeated whatever it was he'd said, and reluctantly Tom replied in the same tones so that none of his friends knew what it was he was saying.

The stranger in the cloak narrowed his eyes and appeared to snap out an order. Tom heaved a sigh and

rolled his eyes. Katie laughed and then realized she
shouldn't have because the stranger glared at her. The
man snapped out another order, and this time Tom took
a deep breath and then began to recite. The words came
out of him hesitantly at first and then faster and louder
until they were tumbling in a cascade of sounds that
broke against the ears of the villagers and then drained
away into the parched ground without leaving a trace of
meaning behind.

At length the man in the cloak held up his hand and
Tom said, 'Oh! I was just getting to my favourite bit!'
But the stranger had turned his horse around and the
three intruders galloped off, leaving the villagers to
cough in a cloud of dust.

'What did he say?' The villagers were clustering around Tom.

'Were you speaking Latin?'

'Does the Abbot want you to be taught in his school?'

'Just think – you could be an Abbot! A Bishop!'

Only Old Molly said nothing, and Tom looked around all those eager faces and shrugged:

'What a skinflint! He gets me to recite a poem and then doesn't offer me a farthing for it! I bet he'd charge you for the holes in your cheese!'

Some time later, Old Molly had sat the two children on the bench outside the cottage with a bowl of soup. Then she had gone to feed the geese.

Tom looked across at Katie.

'What's the trouble?' she asked.

'I'm going to have to run away,' said Tom.

Katie took another spoonful of soup and pretended to count how many bits of cabbage she could see in it. Eventually she said:

'That's silly.'

'No it isn't,' replied Tom. 'It's terrible.'

'Then why do it?'

'That man,' Tom paused to think about the man and shivered. 'He said I was to be the Abbot's scholar.'

'Is that so terrible?'

'It is for me.'

'Then don't go.'

'They're going to make me. It's all the priest's fault for teaching me to read and write . . .'

'But you're brilliant at it!' exclaimed Katie.

'I can't help that,' replied Tom. 'It's not what I want to do.'

'I know what you want to do,' said Katie, 'but that's impossible.'

She looked hard at her brother, and he somehow seemed to find a clump of nettles under the bench more interesting than their conversation.

'Going to the Abbot's school and becoming a churchman isn't a chance many boys get. You ought to be grateful.'

'You're right, of course,' said Tom. 'You're always right, my little Katie.'

He reached over and tousled her hair – just as he had when they were very small and their father had come to the door of their cottage looking pale and told them in a whisper Tom could still hear that their mother had died.

'And when you put it so clearly,' Tom went on, 'I know I've got no choice. No choice at all. I've got to do the impossible.'

· 2 ·

Now running away from home in the fourteenth century was by no means an easy thing to do. Everyone in the village would know exactly who you were and would know that you were supposed to be studying with the parish priest or helping Odo dig a ditch in the Bottom Pasture. Nobody would be sitting inside watching television: they were all outside – all the hours of daylight God sent – in the fields, around the village well, washing in the stream, scrubbing clothes together by the church wall, spinning, mending hedges, or minding the sheep and cattle.

No one was invisible in their own village.

By the same token, Tom knew that as soon as he got to another village, he would be even more visible. He would have become a stranger – an object of interest or suspicion. He certainly couldn't expect to walk through a strange place without explaining who he was and where he was going.

As for waiting for nightfall to make his escape . . . well that was another matter altogether. Night was night in those days. No street lights. Not much light even in the houses, except on special occasions. Dark was dark, and unless there were a moon, you couldn't see one foot in front of you.

Besides, there were wolves in the Great Forest.

'You'd soon have them eating out of your hand,' said Katie, who was wrapping a few pieces of bread in a cloth.

'Don't be daft!' said Tom, 'They'd have my hand off before I could climb a tree and hurl the great boulders at them.'

'Why would you throw boulders at the monks?'

'I'm talking about the wolves,' replied Tom, who in his mind was already escaping from a snarling, starving creature with vicious fangs that even now were ripping at the seat of his breeches.

'Well I was talking about the monks.' Katie sounded a bit hurt. 'They'd like you.'

'I'm not going to be a monk,' Tom explained for the fifteenth time. 'I'm not going to the Abbot's school.'

'I know,' sighed Katie. 'You're running away.' And she handed Tom the packet of bread.

'Tell Old Molly I'm sorry I couldn't say goodbye,' said Tom.

Katie didn't say anything. She was gazing into a future that hung in front of her like a winter's mist: there was no sunlight and no visible destination.

'Cheer up,' said Tom. 'I'll send you word.'

But Katie was crying.

'Oh, Tom!' she said. 'What's going to happen?'

Tom held her away from him and looked into her eyes and grinned.

'Everything!' he said. 'It's *all* going to happen!'

And, in a way, he was right.

*

The ditch was not the first place Tom would have chosen. It was still wet and muddy, despite the hot summer. But he had had no choice. The Reeve was riding towards him, looking around in his usual commanding manner.

'Hey you!' Tom suddenly heard the Reeve shout. His heart leapt into his stomach, his stomach leapt into his throat and then all three – heart, stomach and throat – seemed to shoot together up into his brain, and he had to stop himself peering out of the ditch to see if the Reeve was talking to him.

But the Reeve was talking to Odo.

'They need more men on the other side of Peckarman's and the Five Acre,' he was saying.

'Oh, just give me a crust of bread, Master, and let me lick the leavings in your bowl, and I'll do anything,' cried Odo, tugging his forelock.

'Shut up, Odo,' replied the Reeve.

'It will be an honour to shut up for you, sir,' Odo went on. 'Shall I shut up at once, sir? Or in a few minutes – after you've gone?'

The Reeve must have decided it wasn't worth staying around to be ridiculed, for Tom heard him ride off. And then he heard Odo start humming a little tune to himself.

'Psst! Odo!' whispered Tom.

Odo looked up slowly as Tom emerged from the ditch.

'Ah! Solomon the Wise in a ditch!' said Odo. 'So you're running away?'

'How do you know?' asked Tom.

Odo grinned. 'I heard the Abbot had sent his man round to hear you recite in Latin, so I knew you'd be on your way soon. And you don't normally hide in the ditch when the Reeve comes by.'

'You won't tell anyone, will you, Odo? Just tell Old Molly I'm sorry. And look after Katie.'

Suddenly Odo held up his spade to the sun and clutched his forehead.

'Wait! Wait!' he exclaimed. 'The Great Odo foresees all! He foresees trouble ahead for Young Thomas. He foresees long journeys. New faces. And a wet patch on the seat of his breeches where he lay in the ditch.'

Tom gave Odo a friendly kick.

'Shut up, Odo,' he mimicked the Reeve.

Then they both looked at each other for a moment.

'*You* know why I'm going, don't you?' Tom asked.

Odo didn't reply, but he slipped his hand into his jerkin and suddenly he was holding out a bright object to Tom. It was something that took Tom's breath away for a moment.

'Go on – take it,' said Odo. 'You may need it.'

Tom swallowed, and for the first time the full enormity of what he was doing hit him like a blow in the stomach.

'Take it,' said Odo. 'It's all I've got to give you.'

Tom hesitated. For a moment he felt his stomach was the Well at the World's End, down which he was falling, and there at the bottom he could glimpse shapeless horrors, fears, formless monsters, and he smelt foreign lands that were beyond his imagining. And all the while he heard Katie's cries high up above him, getting fainter and fainter, but there was no going back.

Then he nodded to Odo, and took the knife.

At the brow of Hound Tor, Tom turned and looked back at the village he had known all his life. From up here he could see into all the tofts – the farmyards immediately around the village houses. When you walked through the village, you could hardly see a single house, because of the high banks that separated the tofts from the road. The occasional bridge across the dyke often afforded the only glimpse into these private places.

But from up here on the Tor, Tom could see the figures of the womenfolk as they bustled about from house to hen-house, byre to barn, feeding animals or preparing food for their men, whom Tom could see, even now, toiling in Sir William's fields.

Their own strips of land, that ran under the toft-hedges, would have to wait until the lord's harvest was home. Then it would be all rush-rush and help-thy-neighbour to get their own corn cut before the weather broke.

Tom knew it all, for that was the way things were.

Tom also knew that he had to get well away from the Manor and Sir William's men. If they caught him within four days, he could be hauled back to stand trial as a runaway before the Manor Court.

Another thing that Tom knew was that someone had a tight hold on the back of his neck. He could hear the person breathing rather hard, and he knew who it was.

'Well so much for the Grand Escape!' he said to himself. 'I thought I might have got a bit further than my own village . . . Even a few feet down the road would have counted as a *bit* of an escape . . . whereas this isn't – strictly speaking – an escape at all . . .' But a voice interrupted his chain of thought.

'Thomas! Thomas! What foolishness are you up to now?' The priest had sold his dog and was on his way home.

Tom squirmed, but the priest's bony fingers gripped him hard.

'I'm running away,' gasped Tom.

'Running away from what?' asked the priest.

'I'm not running away *from* anything,' replied Tom. 'I'm running away *to* something!' And with a twist he escaped from the priest's grip and was racing down the hill as fast as his legs could keep up with his feet.

The priest set off after him, but had gone no more than a couple of steps before he fell over and struck his elbow on a stone.

'Ow!' cried the priest.

'Sorry!' yelled Tom over his shoulder. Then Tom stopped and turned. He walked back a few paces to where the priest was lying on the ground.

'I meant to say,' said Tom, 'thank you for all you tried to do for me.'

'Tom!' cried the priest. 'I won't let you go!'

14

'You'll have to stop me,' replied Tom.

'Tom!' yelled the priest, 'Sir William's men will find you – wherever you are! They'll drag you back! They'll force you to work in the fields all day and every day – you'll never get any time to study with me any more! Tom! The books we could have read!'

But Tom was gone. He was off over the stile and across the fields.

'Tom!' the priest was yelling behind him.

Tom shut his eyes as he ran.

'That's torn it!' he was thinking. 'He'll raise the devil and all his legions! I'll never make it!'

Tom felt the hair on the back of his neck prickle as now he heard a horn sounding, and, glancing over his shoulder, he could just see the Reeve himself riding up from the Ox Lease in the distance.

'Damn!' said Tom. 'Damn! He's raised the hue and cry before I'm anywhere!'

Tom looked at the way ahead and took stock.

'The priest will tell the Reeve everything – sure as I'm a fruit-cake!' he told himself. 'They'll catch up with me before I reach Grimscote.'

He had planned crossing the fallow fields to Beasley's Common and then heading for the open road to the next village to the south.

'All right, Thomas,' said Tom to himself. 'It'll have to be Plan B.'

He hadn't wanted to use Plan B, and even as he decided to follow it he felt himself go weak at the knees.

'Plan B is *not* a good plan,' he reminded himself. 'But there's nothing else for it.'

He glanced round. The Reeve was nearly up to Hound Tor, and the priest was running down the hill towards him.

Even so, the idea of Plan B filled Tom with such foreboding that he found himself wondering how fast he would have to run to get clear of the horsemen, but even as these thoughts went scrambling through his mind, he heard another sound that made him turn and run. He didn't even stop to look. He knew what was happening. He could hear the hounds. By some stroke of ill fate, Sir Willliam's men must have been riding past when the Reeve started blowing his horn, and now they appeared over the next hill, riding toward Hound Tor.

Tom ran in sheer panic. His dread of Plan B evaporated in the sweat that broke out all over his body, as he ran towards the Great Wood.

· 4 ·

In those days the Great Wood was exactly that. It stretched from one shire to the next, and you could walk for a week before reaching the sunlight on the other side. There were stories of children who had strayed into it and been lost for ever. Old Molly told tales about Wild Men living in the darkest recesses of the deep forest, who ate tree bark and roots and who never saw God's sunlight except between the branches or glimpsed through the roof of leaves.

'They grow hair on their eyelids,' she used to tell the children, 'and they howl when the sun goes down because they have no God to comfort them.'

'And do they eat small children?' Tom remembered Katie asking.

'Oh, bless your pretty little head,' Old Molly had laughed so the firelight shone off her tooth. 'I suppose they eat anything they can get their hands on, but you needn't be afraid, dearie, they never leave the wild wood, so you're quite safe as long as you don't go into it.'

Tom wished he could say the same for himself as he vaulted a ditch and started on the long hill up to the Great Wood's edge.

'With me it's the other way round. I'm not going to

feel safe until I *do* get into the Great Wood!' he muttered to himself.

The hounds had started baying, and he could hear the raised voices of Sir William's men quizzing the priest. They were calling him a 'lack-land' and a 'popesman', not because they thought he was either of those things, but just because they enjoyed insulting him.

Tom could not actually hear what they were saying, but he could make out the harsh voice of the Reeve occasionally cutting through the others.

'The question is,' said Tom to himself, 'will they take the hounds back to the cottage to put them on to my scent or will they just come straight after me? I know what I'd do in their shoes: I'd split the party. Send a couple of horsemen to head me off before I get to the Great Wood, while the rest go back to the cottage to sniff my old breeches.'

'Hi! Hi! Hi!' echoed across the fields, accompanied by 'Yo! Yo! Yo!' and the sounds of horses separating.

'Devil in carnations!' grunted Tom. 'That's exactly what they *are* doing! Why don't I keep these bright ideas to myself!'

He was gasping now, as the hill began to hold his legs back. The Great Wood loomed ahead of him – perhaps a furlong away. At that precise moment Tom was out of the sight of his pursuers, but he knew it would only be a matter of seconds before they breasted the ridge and would have him in full view.

'A horse can gallop five times as fast as I can run and they're only twice as far behind me as I've got to go . . . Oh! oh! Doesn't pay to be too clever!' Tom could feel his knees going weak as the realization swept over him that he could never make it to the wood – no matter how hard he ran – and his energy seemed to drain out of him . . .

'Come on, legs!' he shouted. 'Keep going!'

But the wood seemed as far off as ever and the hill steeper than it had been, and as Tom glanced over his shoulder he saw the heads of the riders appearing over the ridge.

'They shan't catch me! They shan't catch me!' He wasn't crying, but he knew he would the moment he stopped running. He could almost feel the shock waves from the hooves as the men caught sight of him and kicked their horses into a gallop.

Now Tom's lungs seemed to close off . . . his feet became stones – two dead weights that dragged him back rather than pushing him on up the hill . . . His eyes filled with salty water, but you wouldn't have dared to call them tears. And despite it all, he kept going. His anger forced one foot in front of the other, though the Great Wood seemed as far away as the Court of Prester John. Prester John . . . Kublai Khan . . . Saladin . . . Ogadai . . . Alexander Nevski . . . Marco Polo . . . A world he had never seen, that had seemed within his reach that morning, as he took the bread from Katie and dried her eyes, now seemed to be receding behind the Great Wood, never to be seen or touched or felt . . . dusty tents on the plains of Asia . . . the walls of Antioch . . . Constantinople glittering in the sun . . . the frozen wastes of Russia . . . all there waiting for him . . . and he couldn't even reach the wood that marked the boundary of his own village.

Then the miracle happened.

At least, even if it wasn't a miracle it had the same effect as one. And the odd thing is that Tom himself didn't even know exactly what it was that happened. He wasn't looking. His eyes were fixed on an imaginary castle that had been floating just above the topmost branches of the highest elms but was currently disintegrating and collapsing before his mind's eye. All he heard was a yell and a horrible whinny, and when he looked round he saw the closest of his pursuers sprawled in the ditch that Tom had jumped without even thinking and the horse rolling with its legs in the air. The second horse was rearing up to avoid the first and its rider was clutching on for dear life.

Tom didn't stop to enquire whether the horse had caught a fetlock in a fox-hole or whether anybody had a headache, he suddenly felt all the energy return to his limbs and the hill seemed to flatten out as he flew up it towards the sanctuary of the Great Wood.

Before the horse had stopped rearing, Tom was swallowed up in the dank shade.

The moment Tom had gone, Katie had felt an ache inside. She kept thinking she'd mislaid one of her legs or that a hand had gone missing. Old Molly watched her go about her everyday tasks and said nothing.

And then suddenly it wasn't their cottage any more. The hounds and horses were filling the enclosure and three of Sir William's men had burst into the cottage as if it were a stable. Old Molly sat on the one chair and kept silent. Katie grabbed one of the men by the arm without any clear idea of what she was going to do, and found herself flying across the kitchen floor and cracking her head against the old cauldron which still had a little soup in the bottom.

One of the men had already climbed the ladder up to the loft and called out: 'These'll do!'

He reappeared with Tom's old breeches. Katie struggled to her feet and ran at the man again as if she were trying to snatch Tom's things back. But she was really just getting rid of her anger, and she was still pummelling the man's side as he held her by the hair with one hand and held the breeches up by the other and called the hounds.

That night Katie and Old Molly looked at each other in the fading fire-flicker, and Old Molly nodded. 'He would have made a handsome bishop,' was all she said.

J/22,203

Tom stumbled through the bracken – but although he was trying to keep his legs going as fast as he could, he was trying to slow his mind down.

How could he have got it so wrong?

He'd always known it would be hard to get away from the village without being spotted, but all he needed was a few hours start and then he stood a chance of keeping out of reach of Sir William's men.

Instead of which, here he was caught up in the Great Wood with a hue and cry on his heels. He stopped to catch his breath.

'Marks out of ten for achieving first objective?' he said to himself. 'Nil. Current estimate of likelihood of walking down the gold-lined streets of Constantinople ...?' But before he could offer himself a reasonable estimate Tom heard a sound that sent his mind spinning in an altogether different – and much closer – direction. The sound also made his skin creep.

It wasn't much of a sound, and if he'd heard it when he'd been lying in the meadow in the sunlight with Katie, it wouldn't have worried him in the slightest. It was a dry 'snap'.

'If trees could walk around holding hands,' thought

Tom, 'that's exactly the sort of sound you'd hear all the time. But they don't. You only get that sound when something that *can* move around *is* moving around . . .'

Again his train of thought was interrupted – this time by a rustle in the bushes and the sound of something drawing nearer through the undergrowth.

Suddenly Tom became acutely aware of two eyes staring at him – even though he couldn't see them. He could feel them boring into the back of his neck. And the image of a nose wrinkling up as it caught his scent came into his mind, followed closely by a vivid vision of sharp teeth.

'Time I saw another bit of the forest,' said Tom to himself and he broke into a run, leaping over ferns and fallen logs and undergrowth. His legs were slashed by thorns and bracken and his feet caught in hollows and tangled roots. But Tom didn't notice, for another, different sound had just wiped all other thoughts from his mind. And this new sound didn't just make his skin creep: it made his skin leap about three feet in the air, pulling all his blood and bones with it! It was a long drawn-out howl.

'Wolves!' gulped Tom, and the world became a blur of tree trunks and branches, whipping his face and punching his arms as if the forest had turned into a bully and could do anything it liked with him now it had him at its mercy.

Another howl sent a thrill through every nerve in his body. He crashed and ran and stumbled through the ever-thickening gloom of the trackless forest . . .

How long he ran in this way Tom had no idea. It could have been ten minutes, it could have been ten hours. Time had nothing to do with it. The only thing that he was aware of was the howling and snapping at his back, and the single question that kept repeating and repeating in his mind: why weren't they getting any closer?

He was sure any wolf could easily outrun him through that wild wood. 'And a starving wolf,' Tom found himself adding, 'could probably catch me up in a couple of strides.' And yet the howls didn't get any closer. They didn't get any further away either – they just stayed the same distance behind him, and the expected leap through the foliage and the claws of a ravening animal on his back dragging him over and the slavering jaws snapping at his face never happened.

Tom just ran and jumped and staggered and the howls followed him.

Eventually, however, the inevitable happened: Tom caught his foot in an ivy root and fell sprawling into a thicket of thorns. He shut his eyes and said what you might think was an odd thing: 'Sorry, Katie' – and he waited to be devoured alive.

But still nothing happened. His heart raced. His short life rushed through his head like a storyteller's résumé of yesterday's tale. His hands grasped the thorn bush as if it were his saviour. And – very definitely – nothing happened.

After a moment, he realized there was no more howling or barking. Just the silence of the old forest that had stood there, presiding over the life and death of the creatures beneath its branches, since Time set foot upon the land.

Tom opened his eyes. Dusk was settling down through the lower layers of leaves. He didn't dare turn around. But he knew he had to. He also knew what he would see: a lone wolf . . . a hungry female . . . separated from the pack . . . desperate . . . prepared to attack on its own. He needed a weapon.

And suddenly Tom remembered the gift – the gift that Odo had given him. In a flash, his fingers found the knife and he whirled round as desperate as the wild animal he must confront . . .

Except . . . that it wasn't a wolf. In fact it wasn't a wild animal at all. It was a man.

It was definitely a man, and yet . . . he *looked* like a wolf. His eyes glittered in his head, small and beady. His snout was long and wrinkled up as he sniffed the air. His ears seemed to sit strangely high and pointed on his head, and, every now and again, he licked his lips and displayed a row of sharp yellow teeth.

Tom's relief that it wasn't a wolf lasted approximately half a second.

'The Wild Man of the Woods!' gasped Tom. 'I thought Old Molly was making all those stories up!' But here he was, standing a few feet away from him – even if he didn't have hair on his eyelids. Tom's eyes went wide with terror:

'Look out!' he yelled. 'There's a bear behind you!'

He knew it was an old routine – but it sometimes worked. The Wild Man, however, didn't so much as flick his eyes to one side. He kept them on Tom . . . as if he were memorizing a tasty meal before devouring it.

'But you don't eat children, do you?' Tom found himself talking automatically. It was a habit he'd always meant to cure himself of.

The man's thin lips split into a thin smile – showing his yellow teeth for a brief moment. 'Dangerous,' he hissed. It was almost as if he were searching for the long-hidden memory of a word. 'Dangerous . . . the Wood . . .' He pointed at Tom as if to say: 'For you.' But he said: 'Now.'

'I told Katie you didn't,' replied Tom. 'I said Old Molly just made the whole thing up out of her head – well, obviously she didn't make *you* up out of her head, but the bit about you eating . . . oh . . .' The words died on Tom's lips, for the man had now approached him and was peering into his eyes from a few inches away. Suddenly he stubbed a bony finger into Tom's chest.

'You . . .' he hissed, 'with me.'

Then he turned on his heel and plunged back into the undergrowth exactly where the bear hadn't been.

Tom thought for all of a second.

'I could go with him and get eaten alive. Or I could stay here and get eaten alive,' he said to himself. 'On the whole, I think I'd prefer to have the company.' And he made his way after the man as fast as the forest would let him. They ran downhill into a dell through which a brook meandered. The man leapt into the stream and began to run along it as if it were a road.

'At least this'll throw the hounds off the scent,' thought Tom to himself.

'That's why we are,' said the man without looking back.

'Oh . . . right!' said Tom.

Some time later Tom was trying to remember whether he'd spoken aloud about the hounds or merely been thinking about them, when he found he'd arrived at the strange man's even stranger home in the wood.

The first strange thing Tom could see about it was that you couldn't really see it. You could tell it was there because the forest became impossibly thick at that point, but where the upright logs of the cabin began and the tree trunks of the forest stopped was anybody's guess. The second strange thing about the log cabin was that it seemed to be alive. All the logs supported branches that in turn held out green leaves. And the roof was not the usual dark thatch – it appeared to be a thick canopy of leaves – just as if the whole thing were growing out of the forest floor.

But Tom hadn't yet seen the strangest thing of all.

As they approached, the man gave a low whistle and out of the cabin door came one . . . two . . . three . . . four . . . five . . . six . . . seven . . . sleek, grey creatures. The hair on the back of Tom's neck rose. 'If those dogs weren't dogs,' he thought to himself, 'I'd swear they were wolves.'

'*Are* wolves!' snapped the man, and he fixed his beady eye on Tom – sending Tom's mind spinning back to yet another of Old Molly's stories:

'Once there lived in the forest,' she would say, 'a man who loved wolves. He understood their ways. He knew how to speak with them. And he used to live among them just as if he were a wolf himself. People called him the Wolfman . . .'

'Dogs!' said the Wolfman, with some contempt, and then suddenly barked and snapped like an animal so that Tom jumped out of his skin, and would probably have turned and run away were it not for the fact that when he did turn, he found one of the wolves had been sniffing around the back of his breeches and was only now backing off under the Wolfman's threats.

Tom felt like a mouse who finds himself an honoured guest at a cats' dinner. Each wolf seemed to be eyeing him hungrily, and the Wolfman himself no less. 'Maybe they're waiting for me to make a break for it,' thought Tom. 'They probably enjoy a little chase before supper . . .'

But before he could develop a coherent theory about giving the wolves indigestion by not providing them with adequate exercise before their evening meal, Tom noticed a sword flying through the air towards him. 'Gosh, it's lucky I noticed that sword the Wolfman's just thrown at me, because it means I have a reasonable chance of getting out of its way.' But even as he jumped, the sword twisted in the air and Tom had caught it by the handle as if that's what he'd always intended.

A bit non-plussed, Tom stood there, sword in hand, and watched while the biggest of the wolves rose to its feet.

'I wish someone would tell me what's going . . .' But Tom never finished the sentence (he was probably going to say 'on') because the great wolf had leapt at him and Tom was now flat on his back with four paws on his chest and the jaws of a wolf six inches from his face.

'This is a bit rum,' thought Tom. 'But the rummest thing is that I'm not scared . . .Come on! Get scared!' he told himself. 'You've got a wolf standing on your chest! I order you to be scared at once!' But he wasn't. He looked into the wolf's eyes, and he knew that no harm would come to him.

'Why don't you use the sword?' The voice of the Wolfman was suddenly hissing in his ear.

'What? Oh! the sword!' exclaimed Tom. 'Isn't that a bit dangerous?'

Before he knew it, the wolf was off his chest and the others were all sitting about him, barking and baying, while the Wolfman growled and snarled back at them. This din went on for some time, until eventually the Wolfman clapped his hands and the others fell silent. He then turned on Tom and smiled:

'My friends say they think you can be trusted,' he said.

Tom was just about to reply that he wasn't sure whether that was the point – so far as he was concerned the point was could *he* trust seven huge timber wolves – especially when it came to supper time. But somehow he found himself saying 'Thank you,' and he knew that he had just undergone a test of some sort and passed.

That night, Tom slept surrounded by wolves.

'I wouldn't exactly call this "sleeping",' muttered Tom as he lay listening to the breathing of the animals and smelling the sweetish odour of their bodies. 'I mean how do I know that – as soon as I've nodded off – one of these beasts won't just roll over and gobble me up?' But he knew he was now one of their number.

· 8 ·

The next day he was up with the Wolfman at first light, running silently through the dripping wood, with the wolves at their side. The little sunlight that penetrated the gloom of the Great Wood had not risen above the bracken when they surprised a wild boar. It reared up, and crashed its way through the forest, and the wolves and the Wolfman and their feet suddenly took wings. Tom found himself floundering on his own as his grey companions flung themselves into the chase and were gone.

Tom heard no baying from the pursuers; he heard no roaring from the hunted. But some time later, when he came across his comrades in a clearing, the boar was already skinned and the Wolfman was cutting up the carcass ready to transport it back to his cabin. The wolves were rewarding themselves with the choice offal.

That night Tom watched the Wolfman set up some of the meat to smoke over a hazelwood fire behind the hut, and the rest was cut up into strips to dry in the wind. One haunch, however, had been set over the camp-fire itself to roast, and soon they were settling down to their first meal.

The Wolfman looked over to Tom and said: 'Where?'

For a moment Tom was nonplussed.

'Run away,' said the Wolfman.

'Yes,' said Tom.

'Not a thief,' observed the Wolfman.

'No. I'm not a thief,' agreed Tom.

'Why?' asked the Wolfman. A simple eagerness animated his eyes.

'Why?' asked Tom. 'Because I have read books.'

'Books!' said the Wolfman. 'Latin.'

'Well, yes – there aren't any books written in English. But the priest taught me . . . I can do it standing on my head . . . I don't know why – that's just how things are. But I've read *books*. I've read of the world that lies beyond the village – beyond the Great Wood even – Arabia . . . Cathay . . . the Land of the Tartars . . . I want to see it . . .'

'Something else,' said the Wolfman, looking up from his meat. 'Another thing.' He said it as a statement of fact. As if he knew.

'No . . .' said Tom and was cut short by a hiss from the Wolfman.

'No lies,' he whispered. 'We are wolves . . . have to trust each other. Must not deceive.'

Tom pretended to concentrate on his eating. But the Wolfman had put down his meat and was leaning across to Tom. 'Something you want but are afraid to name.'

'Yes,' said Tom. 'There is something else.'

The Wolfman waited. But Tom didn't say any more.

That night, as they lay in the darkness of the cabin, the Wolfman told a story, while Tom and the wolves listened and dreamed.

'Once,' said the Wolfman, 'all the wolves ran wild and free. They meant no more, one to the other, than the sticks and stones on the forest floor. Oh! the wolf-mother looked after her cubs and the wolf-father hunted as best he could, but a lone wolf can only bring down small game, and many a cub went hungry.'

One of the she-wolves stirred and growled.

'But one wolf would no more think of helping another than a herring would think of helping a gull. They kept themselves to themselves and if one found another with a carcass to share as like as not they would fight over it.

'Then one year the thing that all wolves dread most happened: the winter never stopped. The ice stayed hanging from the branches and the snow lay on the forest floor itself. The sun stayed hidden from sight, and the Arctic wind howled all day and howled all night. The wolves grew thin, and hunger made them bitter in their bones so they could not bear the sight of one another.

'And so it was that the Great Wolf-Who-Spoke-For-All-Wolves called a parliament of wolves in this very forest. Wolves came from Siberia, they came from Lapland, they came from the Carpathian mountains and gathered here in the Big Clearing, where the river breaks its neck, and there they listened to what the Great Wolf had to say.'

Suddenly Tom found that *he* was telling the story. He didn't know how it happened, but the words kept coming into his head and the Wolfman fell silent and watched Tom as he continued the tale.

'"We are all going to die," said the Great Wolf-Who-Spoke-For-All-Wolves, "if we carry on as we are, for there is not enough small game to live on, and if we fight each other we will waste the little strength that we have left." The wolves sat round, thin and aching, while the Arctic wind blew up the fur on the back of their necks.

'And then,' continued Tom, 'the Great Wolf spoke the words that would change for ever the way of wolves all over the world. "To survive," he said, "we must work together. No wolf to go alone but each with the other, hunting together, living together, help to the helper, each pair of eyes looking out for all. That is the way it must be from now on." Those were the words of the Great Wolf,' said Tom. And as the firelight flickered low, the wolves in the Wolfman's cabin stirred and seemed to huddle closer than they had been.

'And the wolves returned to the frozen wastes of Siberia, to the Carpathian Mountains and the dense forests of the world . . .' It was the Wolfman who had taken up the story again. 'And from that day they hunted in packs, and lived in a society of wolves; and all through that long winter that came from the North and stayed for year upon year, when other creatures starved and died, the wolves multiplied.'

Tom listened to the wind howling through the Great Wood outside the cabin, and he felt strangely safe, surrounded by those grey, sleeping creatures that he had always feared.

Tom lost count of the days. He felt no urge to leave the Wolfman, for he was learning new things every day. He learnt to read the forest floor just as he had learnt to read the pages of books. The tracks of animals, the breaking of sticks, the turning over of leaves – all these things began to speak to him and tell him who had passed that way and when and why. And all the time, he listened to the stories of the wolves and learnt from the things they told him. The Wolfman watched Tom grow into the ways of the forest and learn the language of the wolves, and many a time he shook his head with admiration at the speed with which Tom learnt.

One morning, when Tom was alone in the camp, mending a hole in his breeches, Sweet Grey, the youngest female, came crashing out of the forest with fear in her eyes. In a few barks and growls she blurted out a strange story to Tom. She and Broken Fang had been running together in the forest when Broken Fang had fallen under an enchantment. He could neither speak nor move, backwards nor forwards. Where was the Wolfman? Only he knew of the enchantments of the forest, of the wizard spells and charms and their antidotes.

Tom was up and into his unpatched breeches before Sweet Grey could finish. 'Show where,' he said.

Sweet Grey hesitated. 'We should find the Wolfman,' she said. 'Only he has the key to such magic.'

'The Wolfman won't be back until the sun starts to go down,' said Tom. 'Where is Broken Fang?'

And so, reluctantly, Sweet Grey led Tom through the forest to where Broken Fang was lying. He looked up as Tom approached and bared his teeth, showing the fang he broke when he was a young cub.

'What is the trouble?' asked Tom, but Broken Fang said nothing. Nor did he move. He just lay there.

'He's enchanted!' whined Sweet Grey in Tom's ear. 'Look! He won't move. Magic.'

But Tom was examining one of Broken Fang's feet. 'It's about as magic as the hole in my breeches,' he muttered as he pulled back the bracken and there it was: a man-trap – cold iron teeth sinking deeper and deeper into the hot flesh of Broken Fang's leg. Broken Fang looked at Tom wildly, and Tom realized that the pain and shock had paralysed him.

Without more ado, Tom tried to prise the jaws of the trap open, but the spring was too strong. Broken Fang began to whimper. 'A lever,' said Tom. 'That's what Archimedes would have used!' And the next minute he was scrabbling around the undergrowth looking for a suitable stick.

Sweet Grey watched him with concern: 'Are you leaving him?' she growled.

'Don't worry, Sweet Grey, I wouldn't leave him like this – not for all the fish on Friday! And if I could find whoever set this trap I'd get him to try it out on himself

first . . .' Even as he was speaking, a shock of terror stopped the words on Tom's lips, for he suddenly knew who had set the trap – *and* who it was for . . . But there was no time to think about it; he had to release Broken Fang, and he now realized something that Archimedes would probably have realized from the start – he was never going to find a stick strong enough to open the man-trap.

'Sweet Grey,' said Tom. 'Wait here. I'm going to get help.' And before Sweet Grey could growl her fears of further enchantments and spells, Tom was speeding back to camp. There he seized the one piece of iron in the place – the tripod from which the cauldron hung – and raced back to the two wolves. The next moment he was levering the jaws of the trap apart – enough for Broken Fang to pull his leg free before the jaws snapped shut again.

'Thank you, Archimedes!' Tom yelled.

And now it was as if the enchantment had lifted, for Broken Fang threw back his head and howled with the pain and with the rage against the man who had set such a cruel trap.

Tom meanwhile was examining the injured leg. It was cut through to the bone, and the bone itself was broken. He stopped Broken Fang as the wolf tried to hobble to his feet. Then Tom bent down and heaved the great animal on to his back. Sweet Grey picked up the tripod in her mouth and slowly they made their way back to camp.

By the time the Wolfman returned, Tom had set Broken Fang's leg in a wooden splint, bathed the wound in an in-fusion of bugleweed and foxtail and wrapped it in willow leaves. The Wolfman nodded and busied himself preparing a meal.

That night Sweet Grey kept telling the story again and again: 'It was a man-trap,' she kept saying. 'Bigger than anything I've seen before. Bigger than a wolf snare. Hideous jaws . . . horrible . . . none of us would have thought of what Tom did . . . he didn't even stop to think . . . he knew exactly what to do . . .'

Eventually Tom had to cut her short. 'Forgive me, Sweet Grey,' he said. 'But I have something to say to everyone. I have decided it is time for me to go.'

A silence fell over the wolves. Broken Fang whined. The Wolfman looked at Tom in surprise – and yet he didn't seem to be surprised.

'You heard what Sweet Grey said,' Tom looked around at them. 'It was a man-trap. It could have been set for me. As long as I am here, I am a danger to you.'

'Where to?' asked the Wolfman.

'Where I always planned to go,' said Tom.

The Wolfman screwed up his eyes. 'Still afraid to say your dream?' he asked. Tom was suddenly preoccupied with making sure Broken Fang's leg was properly set in its splint. 'If you cannot tell us, we cannot help you find it,' said the Wolfman.

But how could the Wolfman – living here under the Great Wood, cut off from the world of men – how could he help me in what I want to do? thought Tom.

'Maybe I can,' said the Wolfman, as if he had heard Tom's thoughts like words.

· 10 ·

The next day, Tom was awake at first light, but he found the Wolfman was already up before him. He had prepared two packs and was sitting outside the cabin waiting for him. As soon as Tom stepped out, the Wolfman said: 'Shall we go?'

Tom frowned. 'We?'

'You have learned a lot,' said the Wolfman, 'but not enough to see you through the Great Wood from one end to the other.'

Tom nodded. 'I must say goodbye.' He was just about to go back into the cabin, when his companion stopped him.

'Wolves do not say goodbye. Will meet again.' With that the Wolfman hoisted the pack on to his back, and set off, and Tom had to scramble to keep up with him.

As they made their way through the forest, a curious feeling began to take hold of Tom, although he couldn't at first make out what it was. 'It's not tummy ache,' said Tom to himself, 'and it's not fever. It's almost like exhaustion but I'm not tired . . . It's like something tearing inside me . . . But I'm fine . . . I can't think what it . . .' And then he suddenly realized what it was.

'Loneliness,' he murmured. 'How strange.' And yet

that was undoubtedly what it was. The further they walked away from the camp and the wolves he had grown to trust and rely on, the stronger grew the feeling – of a great loneliness settling over his spirit.

'You are leaving the pack,' explained the Wolfman, as if Tom had been telling him all about how he felt. 'You will have to find the strength within you to be able to be alone again.'

For a moment, Tom felt overwhelmed by all that lay ahead: would the hue and cry still be going? Would Sir William's men still be looking for him? How could he possibly make his way? *Where* should he make his way? And how could he ever hope to become what he wanted, above all else, to *become*?

'Stop that!' Tom told himself severely. 'That sort of thinking is about as useful as a dry duck pond.' And he quickened his pace so that he was walking closer behind the Wolfman.

That night they camped beside a small stream, and as the fire flickered low and the chill of night nudged them closer to it, the Wolfman leant over to Tom and slipped a small wooden object on a leather thong into his hand.

'What's this?' asked Tom.

But the Wolfman only smiled.

'It's a whistle,' said Tom, and he raised it to his lips, but before he could blow it, the Wolfman had thrust out a hand and stopped him.

'Will bring all the wolves within hearing.'

Tom gasped. 'The Wolf Whistle!' he murmured. 'I thought it was just another story.' He turned the thing over in his hand.

'Now you speak the language of wolves, one day, perhaps, useful.'

'You mean I can keep it?' exclaimed Tom. But the Wolfman had already rolled over and appeared to be asleep, so Tom muttered his thanks to the fire, and hung the whistle round his neck.

The next day they were off again at first light. Deeper and deeper into the Great Wood they went. Glimpses of the sky became as rare as diamonds and light as hidden as a miser's gold. It even seemed as if the air were scarcer this deep in the forest, and Tom was relieved when the canopy above began to thin out again, and the Wood became less dense.

Still they marched on, day after day, until one morning they finally reached the southernmost limit of the Great Wood, and stumbled out into the full light of day.

'There,' said the Wolfman. 'There is your way,' and he pointed to a path that ran along the forest's edge before it veered off and over the hills towards a distant town. 'I hope you find the dream.'

Before Tom had had time to take in the sight before him and had even begun to think of a way to thank the Wolfman, his companion had slipped back into the shadow and the forest had swallowed him up.

'Wolves never say goodbye,' murmured Tom. Then he turned back again to stare at the distant walls and turrets of the city that lay ahead.

'Right, Tom!' said Tom to the only person around who answered to that name. 'You're really on your own now.' And yet the curious thing was that he no longer felt on his own. The feeling of great loneliness had been replaced by something else. He couldn't shake off the feeling that he now had a grey wolf running along on each side of him, as he made his way towards the unknown.

· 11 ·

Tom had never been in a city before.

'But I'm *not* a country bumpkin,' he kept reminding himself as the Great Bell of the City echoed across the countryside. 'I read books. I speak Latin. I know things that most people in that town have no idea of . . .' At this moment he received a sharp blow on the back of the head. Tom fell forward on to a sharp rock that was very conveniently placed if you were wanting to fall on to that sort of thing.

'Ouch!' he groaned. 'Attacked by robbers before I even set foot in the city!' and he looked up at the gates in the city wall that the guards were just closing. Citizens and travellers were hurrying in before they were shut out for the night.

Suddenly Tom felt a pair of hands pulling him up. 'Come on!' said a voice, 'the bell's sounding!'

Tom turned and found a boy a little older than himself holding a football. There was a loud 'CLANG!' 'Uh oh!' said the boy. 'They've shut the first gate.'

It was true. A peddler with a pack on his back and a ragged family were squeezing through as the second gate began to close. By the time Tom had taken all this in, his new acquaintance or attacker – he wasn't quite sure

which – was half-way to the city wall.

'Ask them to wait!' shouted Tom. The boy turned to see Tom still where he was. 'Hurry!' he yelled, but even as he did so, the final gate clanged shut. By the time Tom had caught up with him, the boy was standing at the gate listening to the bolts slamming into their places until morning.

'Just open up for a moment!' the boy was shouting. 'You can't leave us out all night – there are bandits around! and wolves! and it's going to be a stormy night!'

But the bolts kept sliding into place.

'My master will reward you!' the boy yelled, and for a moment there seemed to be a hesitation on the inside, but then the last bolt was banged into position. And the Great Bell fell silent.

The sounds of the city on the other side of the gate seemed to disappear, and all the two boys could hear was the wind that was whistling round the walls, and the noise of clouds skidding across the sky – which, as you know, isn't very loud – even though there was a huge black cloud looming over the horizon.

'My name's Alan,' said the boy.

'That's torn it,' said Tom.

'What? Being called Alan?'

'I mean,' said Tom, 'there's going to be a storm.'

'Situation . . . Alternatives . . . Action!' said Alan.

'My name's Tom,' said Tom.

'That's irrelevant,' said Alan. 'It's neither the situation, an alternative, nor a plan of action. The situation is: we are locked out. Alternatives: 1) find a place to sleep out, 2) find the nearest farm and beg for shelter, 3) *Ah-ha!*'

'For someone who speaks English, you're as easy to understand as a Welshman,' said Tom.

'There's no need to talk like that,' said Alan. 'We've got to decide on a course of action and quickly.' A few drops of rain had begun to spot the ground. 'I vote for number three.'

'If I remember all right,' said Tom, 'number three was *ah-ha!*'

'Bull's eye!' replied Alan.

'Well it sounds better than "*Oh no!*",' said Tom, 'so I'll vote for that too.'

'You're a champion!' exclaimed Alan. 'Keep close to me!' And he set off round the massive stonework of the city walls, as the black cloud covered the sky and turned the dusk to night.

They hadn't got further than you could throw a chicken when the heavens opened. The rain came down as if it were being hurled at the earth by angry gods trying to soak the Underworld. At least that's what Tom thought. In a couple of minutes they were both wet to the skin.

Alan grinned: 'Sorry about hitting you on the head.'

'I wondered when you were going to apologize,' Tom grinned back at him.

'Kicked it a bit too hard,' said Alan, and he threw the ball up and kicked it ahead of them so it disappeared into the darkness and rain. 'First one to find it is the leader,' he yelled and sprinted off after it.

Tom followed and only caught up with Alan in time to see him snapping up the ball.

'Lucky it wasn't you,' Alan said. 'You don't know the way.'

'Where are we going?' gasped Tom, shaking the rain out of his eyes.

'Here,' said Alan, and he hid the football under a pile of leaves. 'Have to pick it up in the morning.'

There was a tree growing close to the city wall. It reached about half-way up, and Alan was by now almost half-way up the tree. By the time Tom had joined him in the branches, both boys were shivering, as the wind redoubled its force. It blasted wet leaves and branches into their faces and lashed the rain against their arms and legs.

'This tree shouldn't be here,' explained Alan. 'The mayor and his council keep deciding to have it cut down, but somehow no one's ever got round to it. Probably because it's the only way in after hours.'

'Are you sure it's the way in?' asked Tom, looking up at the wall that still towered above them. But the only reply he got was a wet slap across the face as the branch Alan had been sitting on sprang back. Alan was already climbing on up.

When they reached the branch that grew out closest to the wall, Tom felt even more uncertain. He watched Alan wriggle his way along it. The branch dipped and then lodged on a bit of stonework. Alan squirmed right to the end until he was able to get his hands on the stone. Then he swung down and was hanging from the stonework, scrabbling with his feet to find a foothold. Almost without pausing he started to work his way cautiously and slowly up the vertical wall, finding first one handhold then another; then a ridge for his foot and then a cleft for his toe.

'Don't worry, Tom!' he shouted without taking his eyes

off what he was doing. 'Where there isn't a foothold, someone's cut one, so it's as easy as falling off a log.'

'As easy as falling off a very high wall,' muttered Tom, as he looked down at the ground that lay uninvitingly far below them, almost lost in the rain-sodden darkness.

'Whoa!' Alan gave a sort of laugh. 'I nearly lost it then! It's this rain's made the stone so slippery.'

'Well, I wouldn't want it to be *too* easy,' said Tom, trying to sound confident. But inside he could feel his stomach turning somersaults, as he clung to the branches of the tree and realized he was no longer shivering from the wind, he was shaking with what could only be described as 'fear'.

'Look, Alan, I'm not much of a climber. I think I'll go for option one and just stay here in this tree all night,' That's what he wanted to shout up at his companion, who was now half-way from the branch to the top of the wall. But Tom didn't say anything. He just held on to the tree with all his strength, and tried to stop himself wobbling off and plunging through the leaves down on to the rock beneath.

After what seemed like enough time to read forty books in Latin, *and* translate them into all the languages in the world as well, Tom saw Alan finally reach the parapet and haul himself over – water cascading off his body and down the wall as he did so. Then he turned and looked down as if expecting to see Tom close behind.

'Where are you?' he called in a whisper. 'Are you all right?'

'Yes,' replied Tom in what was more of a whisper than he had intended.

'Then what are you waiting for?'

'Just got to finish my last will and testament and I'll be right with you,' said Tom. But he couldn't move.

'Hurry,' Alan hissed back. 'The watch will be round any minute!'

Tom had never been to a town before, but he knew all about the night-watch, and he had no wish to be caught by it to be handed back to Sir William's men. So he steeled himself and started to squirm his way along the branch.

'Here we go!' he muttered as the branch sagged down and caught on the wall. 'What goes down doesn't always come up!' But the next minute he found his fingers on the stonework and he was swinging himself forwards.

As his feet hit the wall, he felt his fingers slip from their precarious hold above him.

'Agh!' he yelled.

'Sh!' whispered Alan. 'Are you all right?'

'Just about to fall to my death, but otherwise extremely well, thank you very much,' Tom managed to mutter through clenched teeth. 'No cough. No fever. No broken limbs. A hint of impending doom, perhaps, but nothing to . . .'

'Shut up!' whispered Alan. 'Concentrate on what you're doing.'

Tom, at this precise moment was feeling distinctly dizzy. He'd made the mistake of looking down.

'And don't look down,' whispered Alan helpfully.

Tom wanted to groan, but he didn't dare. He felt any effort on his part – even a groan – might dislodge him from his precarious hold. And meanwhile the rain hammered down on him, as if it were trying to tear him away from the wall.

'I can't do it!' The thought suddenly flashed through his mind, but at that very moment Alan hissed down: 'You *can't* fall off.' And although Tom thought: 'What a stupid thing to say,' he suddenly found himself – in some strange way – believing it.

'I can't fall off!' he told himself, and he put his foot into a higher niche, reached up a hand for the next ledge, and before he knew it, he was heaving himself up the sheer face of the wall. His knees were wobbling and his hands were trembling, but he pulled himself up again and almost grinned to himself.

'So this is how a *fly-on-the-wall* feels,' he muttered. 'If this is '*ah-ha!*' I think I'd rather go for '*oh no!*' after all.' He looked up at Alan, and then he wished he hadn't, for his heart immediately dropped down to below his knees. Alan was no longer there.

'It's the night-watch – he's had to hide!' thought Tom. 'Do I go on? Go back? Or just stay here?' It was at that moment he realized something he probably should have realized long before: he could not go back. It was, quite simply, impossible. Staying where he was was equally out of the question . . . he could feel his strength ebbing away with the rain that washed over him and down the wall. There was only one course of action. Up he went.

'I can't fall off,' he repeated to himself. But somehow, without Alan's face peering down at him Tom no longer quite believed it in the same way, and he felt the dizziness returning and he found himself beginning to think what a relief it would be just to lean right back and fall quietly and gently into the darkness. 'Except that it wouldn't be all that gentle – not when I hit the ground anyway . . . oooh!' and the more he thought about hitting the ground and how *ungentle* that would be the dizzier he got – until he could no longer move. He simply clung to the wet wall, feeling tears beginning to mix with the rain on his cheeks.

'And *now* – to crown it all – I'm crying!' he groaned. He cried with fear and misery and loneliness when something struck him hard on the back of his head.

'Ouch! This is getting to be a habit!' he muttered – although he might just as well have yelled: 'HELP!' for the surprise of being hit on the back of the head while half-way up a city wall had made him lose his footing. Next second his fingers slipped from the stonework and he found himself falling back into space – just as he'd been imagining.

His arms flailed and he reached out as if to grasp thin air, and the thought flashed through his mind: 'If only the air were nice and thick so you could hold on to it or jump into it like you can with a cartload of hay . . . or the water in the duck pond . . .' But before he'd really finished thinking all that, he found his hands had accidentally grabbed the thing that had hit him on the back of the head. It was the knotted end of a heavy rope.

'Sorry!' Alan's face had reappeared over the battlements. 'Didn't mean to hit you.' Tom just hung there, clinging with all his remaining strength on to the rope that Alan had thrown – his feet dangling in space.

'Thank God you did!' was all he could think.

'Climb!' said Alan.

So Tom put his feet on to the wall and hauled himself up with the rope. It wasn't as easy as he'd imagined, but

Tom didn't really think about that, he was concentrating too hard on keeping his grip.

By the time he reached the top, he felt his arms would have dropped off, if Alan hadn't caught him by the jerkin and somehow bundled him up and over the parapet of the city wall.

Tom collapsed, head first, on to the floor, and was surprised to receive a kick from his rescuer.

'It's the watch!' hissed Alan.

'Who's that?' called a man with a lantern, who had just appeared on the ramparts some distance away. So without more ado, the two boys disappeared into the darkness as fast as their legs would carry them, and the night-watchman never discovered who it was. In later years, he would often say to his wife as they sat round the fire: 'I wonder who it was . . .'

'Probably a robber,' his wife would say. 'Just as well you left them alone, dear.'

'I suppose you're right,' the night-watchman would reply, poking the embers of the fire. 'Still, I bet they're having a more exciting life than mine.'

During the day, you see, the night-watchman sold pies.

· 12 ·

It was not until sometime later that Tom and his new friend finally stopped running.

'Stick with me – "Tom" did you say your name was?'

'That's right.'

'I know the tapster at the White Hart – she'll serve us even though it's after curfew.' And before Tom could reply, he found himself following Alan into an inn where several lamps were still burning, and an odd assortment of men were sitting around arguing about the war in France.

Now I have to tell you at this point that Tom had never been in an inn before. At least not a real inn like this; where travellers from distant parts lodged for the night, and where the stable held more than a dozen horses. Back in the village, you could buy ale from Margery Red Cap and you could sit on the bench outside her cottage while you drank it, but an inn – a proper inn – was quite a different thing.

'Now then, young Nigel, what are you doing about after curfew?' The large woman with bright red cheeks, who had just put a jug of ale in front of a man who was asleep, appeared to be addressing Alan.

'Oh, Joan, love of my life,' said Alan, 'me and my

young friend here we've been kept at it that hard by my master – we've only just been able to get away. A jug of ale for pity's sake – and I'll be yours until the sun goes down!'

'The sun's gone down. The curfew's rung. And you've no more been working late for your master than I've been dining with the King and Queen. Look at you! You're both soaked to the skin. Your tongue'll get you into trouble one of these fine days, young Nigel.' The tapster sounded very severe, but somehow her eyes twinkled and the next moment she was off fetching the ale.

'I thought you said your name was Alan,' whispered Tom.

'Did I?' his friend looked at him. 'Well so it is! But it's not always wise to be known too well around town, is it?'

Tom didn't really know, so he said: 'Why do they have a curfew, anyway?'

'Fire regulations,' replied Alan. 'Everyone has to put out their fires, otherwise – well you can imagine if everyone burnt fires all night in a city like this – after all, houses are made of wood, aren't they?'

Suddenly there were two pots of ale in front of them and the next minute Joan was throwing a blanket over their backs. 'You'll catch your deaths you will,' she muttered and went off to another customer's call.

They both stopped shivering after a while, and then began to relax for the first time since they'd met. Tom's mind was racing back over the nightmare climb up the city wall. 'Thanks for getting me up that last bit,' he said, 'but I expect *you* found it pretty hard the first time *you* did it.'

Alan took a swig of ale and licked the froth off his lip. Then he grinned at Tom. 'That *was* the first time,' he said.

'But, I thought . . .' said Tom.

'And tell you what,' added Alan, 'I don't think I'll try it again – it was blooming scary!' Alan laughed and disappeared behind his mug.

'But you said . . . at least you gave the impression that you did it all the time!' cried Tom.

'Well,' said Alan, reappearing for a moment, 'I thought you might funk out otherwise. Well done, by the way. Many fellows wouldn't have made it.'

Tom looked round at the arguing men, at the busy serving girl, at the unfamiliar room, and suddenly, for the first time so far in his adventure, he was gripped by a feeling – almost a dread, almost a hope – that the world might not be at all what he thought it was.

'You got a farthing?' asked Alan.

'No,' said Tom. 'I don't have any money.'

'You're joking!' exclaimed Alan. 'Do you mean to say you've left home without a penny in your pocket?'

'Well, yes,' replied Tom. 'We don't really use money in the village. A pint of ale usually costs a cabbage – give or take a few leaves.'

Alan rolled his eyes. 'This is the most serious situation we've been in since we met,' he said. 'My relationship with Joan depends on me being able to pay for what I drink.'

'Don't *you* have any money?' asked Tom.

'Did,' said Alan. 'Don't any more.'

Tom suddenly felt how pleasant it would be to be curled up on the floor of Old Molly's cottage under his own blanket, warm and safe and miles away from any town.

'Situation . . . Alternatives . . . Action!' whispered Alan. 'The situation is we've just drunk a quart of good ale costing one farthing and we can't pay for it. Alternatives: 1) We tell Joan, she calls the governor and he and his man give us a sound thrashing and then hand us over to the night-watch. *And* – what's worse – I'm never allowed in here again. 2) We find some money. 3) We sneak out.

'Action? Obvious . . .'

'We tell Joan,' sighed Tom.

'We sneak out,' replied Alan.

'We can't do . . .'

But Tom never said 'that', because Alan had already got up and was striding to the door. Once there he paused and said: 'Thanks, Joan. My friend will pay,' and he was gone.

'If that's "sneaking out", I'm a pickled herring,' muttered Tom.

'You take care now, Master Nigel,' Joan was calling after him. 'The night-watch are very busy at the moment.'

Tom sat there – a hot lump rising into his throat. 'I've changed my mind. I'll become a priest after all. I'll sit and read books all day and chant prayers all night.'

Joan was standing in front of him. 'You mind that Nigel,' she was saying.'Have you known him long?'

'No,' said Tom in a very small voice.

'You can't trust a word he says,' Joan went on.

'I already know,' said Tom in an even smaller voice.

'Have you finished the ale?' asked Joan.

'Yes,' said Tom in a voice that was now so small you could have slid it under the doormat.

'So you'll be going?' asked Joan.

Tom's voice was by now so tiny – so infinitesimal – that when he said, 'I haven't any money to pay for the ale,' Joan didn't even realize he was talking to her. So Tom took his courage in both hands and said it louder. 'I haven't any money to pay for the ale.'

Joan heard this time. A frown crossed her face. 'Uh-oh!' thought Tom. 'Here it comes: "HUBERT!" "Yes, Joan?" "Customer can't pay." "Get the horse-whips and

61

the night-watch! Throw him into the city jail!" What a wonderful way to finish my great voyage!' Tom then noticed a rather odd thing. Joan, the tapster, wasn't calling for the governor nor any such thing. She was laughing.

'Lord bless you!' she was saying. 'I never charge Nigel nothing for a little drink – no! nor his friends. You're welcome to a mug of ale now and then. Yes indeed you are!' And she laughed all the way back to the serving-bench.

The bright red that Tom's face had acquired should have drained away immediately, but it didn't. Instead it went through a subtle transformation as it changed from a flush of shame to a flush of rage. 'I'll give that Alan, or Nigel or whatever his name is, a piece of my mind! And not a piece he'll like either! In fact, the most unpleasant piece of my mind I can find! ALAN!' he yelled as he stepped out of the inn. But Alan, or Nigel or whatever his name was, was nowhere to be seen. And suddenly Joan's face appeared at the door.

'Sh! What are you doing, boy? D'you want to call the whole night-watch down on you?' she whispered.

'I forgot,' Tom whispered back.

'How far have you got to go?' asked Joan.

Tom was stumped for an answer. What should he say? 'As far as Constantinople? As far as the deserts of Arabia? Cathay? Lands that lie beyond the imagination of a boy from a tiny village lost amongst the wooded hills of England? Lands that no one in this town has glimpsed even in their dreams? Lands that lie too far away to even talk about on the doorstep of an inn in the blackness of a city night?' But he said nothing.

'Well you mind how you go,' whispered Joan. 'They

62

can be very rough with curfew-breakers, and if they don't know you they'll throw you into jail. Here, you better have a lantern.'

'But they're bound to see me if I carry a lantern!' exclaimed Tom.

'It's against the law to go about at night without one,' replied Joan. 'Oh and don't say you was here!'

The door of the inn closed in Tom's face, and only as he heard the bolts slide across on the other side did it occur to him that he could have asked for a bed on the floor there. 'For an intrepid adventurer,' thought Tom, 'I'm turning out to be a bit of a Willy.' Then he swivelled round and peered into the dark alley-ways and narrow streets of the city.

The light from his lantern played on the wattle-and-daub walls of the houses opposite, and he felt like a beacon, standing there to attract all the night-watchmen in town. 'I might just as well walk around shouting: "Come and get me!" he murmured. 'And if they did, at least I'd have a roof over my head – even if it's just the jail roof.'

It had started to rain again as Tom made his way down the narrow street, not knowing where he was going and not even sure what he was looking for. Many months later, in another land, when the sun was beating down on him so hot that he could barely think and death seemed to be staring him in the face, he remembered this moment in the wet night of the city as the worst – as the lowest point in his career.

'Nothing could ever be worse than not knowing what you're meant to be doing,' he told himself, at which precise moment a voice said: 'Who goes there?' and a night-watchman appeared from the shadows. 'I don't recognize you.'

For an answer, Tom simply dropped his lantern and ran, and the night-watchman ran after him. 'At least I know what I'm doing *now*!' said Tom to himself as he ran down one street and up another and he heard the night-watchman dropping further and further behind. 'He runs about as well as one of Old Molly's suet puddings,' thought Tom, and he felt a rush of confidence which evaporated immediately. The reason for this was a foot that suddenly stuck out of a darkened alley and sent him sprawling on to the road with his face in the gutter. Before he could even splutter, a hand had pulled him up and he'd been yanked forcibly into the alley-way.

A few moments later the night-watchman ran past, puffing and muttering to himself: 'Stupid job this is. I never catch anyone. Might as well be asleep in bed.'

'That always fools him,' said a voice, and Tom found himself face to face with Alan or Nigel or whatever his name was.

'You villain!' cried Tom, punching him in the chest.

'Sh!' whispered Alan.

'You did it deliberately!' exclaimed Tom. 'You never pay at the inn!' And the next minute they were rolling on the ground, wrestling and punching and Alan was laughing and Tom was gasping for breath.

Finally they stopped, exhausted, and Alan said: 'Come on! We'd better get home.' And Tom thought he'd never heard more welcome words in his life.

· 14 ·

Sometime later, Tom found himself in an abandoned house where the thatch had partly fallen in and rain ran down the bare walls.

'Not much of a home, is it?' remarked Tom. The town had been scarred with such ruins ever since the time of the Plague.

'Let's get a fire going,' replied Alan.

'I thought we couldn't light fires after curfew?' said Tom.

'Stop being a Willy and find some wood,' said Alan.

The two boys took off their wet clothes and hung them over the fire to dry. Tom teased Alan for keeping his breeches on, but the elder boy just laughed. Alan then produced a blanket that he had smuggled out of the inn, and the two of them huddled together under it, trying to stop their teeth chattering.

'Where's your home, really?' asked Tom.

Alan snorted: 'Anywhere. Home is a state of mind. That's all. Where's yours?'

'Up north.'

'So Master Tom's run away from home and doesn't know where he's going.'

'Yes I do,' replied Tom.

'Where?'

But Tom didn't reply. The fabled lands of Arabia, Tartary and Cathay had all seemed so real back in the village, but here the rain seemed to have washed the bright images down the city gutters.

'Maybe I don't,' muttered Tom. And before Alan could ask another question Tom was asleep – or at least he appeared to be.

· 15 ·

The next day was a crisp autumn day full of sunshine.

'My master's going to kill me,' said Alan. He looked as if he'd woken up with lead feet, as they dragged themselves through the early morning town.

'Who's your master?' asked Tom.

Alan's reply had an unexpected effect on Tom. It made him jump in the air and start walking backwards, whistling.

'I only said his name is Sir John,' said Alan.

'And you're his squire?' said Tom.

'I should have been cleaning his armour last night,' replied Alan, 'but we had this game of football and . . . well . . . you know the rest.'

'Will I meet him?'

'Stop walking backwards,' replied Alan. 'It makes me nervous.'

Sir John Hawkley was not in a good mood. You'd never have guessed it, apart from the fact that he kept throwing his boots (and anything else that came to hand) at anyone who entered the room – oh! and his face looked as if you could roast chestnuts on it – *and* he was bellowing: 'Satan's boils! I am surrounded by fools and incompetents!'

'That's not us,' whispered Alan. He and Tom were sheltering in the safety of the landing outside Sir John's room, listening to various objects thudding against the door.

'Liars and loafers!' yelled Sir John.

'Ah! That's us!' grinned Alan, and he stuck his head round the door.

'Ralph!' roared Sir John. 'You skiving good-for-nothing bum-warmer! Where were you last night?'

'So your real name's Ralph?' whispered Tom.

'Sh!' said Alan.

'Who's that with you?' yelled Sir John, flinging a pewter mug at Tom. It missed him by a couple of inches and would have whistled out across the narrow landing except for the fact that Tom caught it.

'Quick reactions!' shouted Sir John.

'This is Sam,' said Alan. 'He wants to know if he can join your service.'

Now this was only partly true. It was certainly correct to say that all his life Tom had wanted – more than anything else – to enter the service of a noble knight, to become a squire and learn the use of arms, to wield a sword, to joust, to ride into battle and achieve deeds of glory. This had been his long-held secret that he had kept from everybody – from Old Molly, from the village priest, from Odo, from the Wolfman – the secret that he had only ever dared to share with his sister Katie. They both agreed it was impossible, but Tom knew he had to try.

That was all beyond dispute. But confronted by the scowling, red-faced Sir John, who had just leapt across the meanly furnished lodging-room and cuffed Alan so hard about the head that he had fallen into Tom's arms, Tom wasn't at all sure that he wanted to enter the service of this *particular* noble knight.

'Get that scoundrelly, trustless, good-for-nothing out of my sight before I tear his liver out with my bare hands and eat it for my breakfast!' Tom suddenly realized that Sir John was addressing him.

'Yes, Sir John!' he exclaimed and pulled Alan back through the door. The moment it slammed shut, Tom had the most curious feeling that somehow – whether he liked it or not – he had already joined the service of Sir John Hawkley.

'Phew! Got away with that all right, didn't we?' said Alan or Ralph or Nigel, nursing his ear.

'Did we?' asked Tom.

'You go in and start cleaning his armour. I'll lie low until he's cooled down a bit.'

Tom thought this over. It took him a couple of seconds to reach the conclusion that whatever his misgivings about entering the service of Sir John, he had no immediate alternative. 'If you're choosing between something and nothing,' Tom said to himself, 'always choose *something*.' And so that was what he did. If he hadn't made that decision I probably wouldn't be writing this story, you wouldn't be reading it, and Tom would never have gone through all the trials and troubles and adventures that lay in store for him.

'But I must know one thing,' said Tom to his friend. 'What do I call you?'

'Alan of course.'

'But Sir John calls you Ralph.'

'So?'

'And at the inn you're called Nigel.'

'Listen,' said Alan, Ralph, Nigel. 'You surely don't imagine you're the same person to everyone who knows you?'

'Of course I am!' exclaimed Tom.

70

'Nonsense!' returned his companion. 'To your little sister you're her big brother, a senior figure, and a source of authority. To Joan at the White Hart you're a small boy up from the country. To me you're a friend.'

'Am I?' said Tom.

'Seems like it.'

'Then I'll call you Alan,' said Tom. 'But how did you know I had a little sister?'

'A lucky guess,' said Alan, and he was off down the stairs. 'I'll be at the inn,' he said, and was gone.

· 16 ·

Tom pushed open the door of Sir John Hawkley's lodging-room with an odd sensation in his stomach – as if he'd eaten a red-hot coal and someone were now trying to pull it back up out of his throat with a pair of tongs.

'Well, get a move – what was your name? Sam?' yelled the great man.

Tom wasn't at all sure why Alan had said his name was Sam. 'Actually it's Tom,' he ventured.

'Sam suits you better,' replied the noble knight. 'Get that stuff clean.' He pointed to a wooden box that stood in a corner of the room. 'We leave for Sandwich tomorrow, Sam.'

'Sandwich?' asked Tom.

'Don't tell me that rapscallion, thief of a squire of mine didn't tell you?'

'I don't think so,' said Tom.

'We join the King's *chevauchée* – we're going to France! I'll be at the inn.' And Sir John was off out of the door before Tom could say: 'Hang on! I don't quite understand. Am I now in your service? What as? How do you know I haven't got other things to do? Why are we going to France? What's a *chevauchée*? Can I learn to become a squire? Am I really coming too? And, finally, why do you want me to clean a box full of sand?' For that was what the box in the corner was full of.

'I suppose he must want me to throw the sand out,' said Tom to himself, 'and then clean the box. Maybe it's a sort of earth-closet.' Tom smelt the boxful of sand. It smelt fine. Then he tried to pick it up. It was so heavy he dropped it almost as soon as he'd lifted it from the floor, and there was a curious sort of muffled 'chink' from inside the sand.

Tom took another cautious smell of the sand, and then, having reassured himself once again that it was not any kind of sewage disposal system, he plunged his hand into it. Immediately he encountered something cold and metallic. He jerked it up and found himself holding a finely wrought coat of mail. Each ring was riveted and linked into the rings around it – like some giant's iron knitting.

Tom had seen mail shirts on Sir William's men, and on the occasional soldiers who had appeared in the village, but he had never touched the stuff before. It was both stronger and more delicate than he had imagined. And it was heavy.

'Of course,' he remembered, 'the sand keeps it clean – sort of scours off the rust.'

There were, however, quite a few patches of rust still clinging to the mail, so he put it back in the box and stirred it around in the sand for some time. When he took it out again the mail had begun to shine – just as if he'd been polishing it.

'It's not quite what I thought being a squire would be like,' thought Tom as he shook the box of sand again, 'but I suppose it's a start.'

*

In fact nothing was quite what Tom thought it would be like. Nothing at all. Not being a squire. Not riding through France. Not fighting for the King. Not surviving the deserts of Arabia. Not being captured by the Saracens. Not ... but we are getting ahead of the story.

At this precise moment the thing that wasn't what Tom thought it would be like was riding in the retinue of a noble knight to join the King's army at the port of Sandwich.

For a start, Tom was walking. For another thing, Sir John Hawkley had a surprisingly modest retinue: it consisted of no more than his good self, Alan his squire, and Tom his – whatever-it-was-he-was. Sir John was mounted on a horse that had a curious way of wheezing whenever it was required to take more than a few steps. Alan was leading a small donkey on which were

strapped all of Sir John's possessions. Tom was carrying
a spear as well as some extra luggage which couldn't fit
on the donkey.

Another thing that was not at all as he'd imagined
was the fact that it was raining. 'Why is it,' thought
Tom to himself, 'that whenever you picture yourself
travelling to strange parts and so on – even when you
imagine the worst possible disasters – it's always
sunny?' As he thought this, the water trickled down his
neck. Sir John wore a wide-brimmed hat, and Alan
wore another. All Tom had was his woollen hood or
'snood' and that didn't keep the rain out.

'Keep up, boy!' yelled Sir John. 'What d'you think
you're doing – taking a Sunday stroll?'

'Sorry, Sir John,' murmured Tom, and he ran a few
paces, but the heavy baggage and the muddy road made
it difficult.

Alan grinned across at him and said: 'Shall we have chicken tonight?'

'We should be so lucky!' exclaimed Tom.

'A noble knight like Sir John eats chicken whenever he wants,' said Alan, 'and so does his retinue.'

'Wow!' said Tom. It was not a particularly intelligent thing to say, but on reflection Tom decided it expressed his feelings exactly. Tartary, Arabia and the Steppes of Russia were all familiar places in his mind's eye, but the idea of eating chicken whenever you wanted was almost beyond his comprehension. For Tom, chicken was a once-a-year treat if you were lucky; to eat it every week or every day would have been pure science fiction – if such a thing had existed.

They had just glimpsed a church spire in the distance. 'There's Sittingbourne,' cried Sir John, 'or I'll be hung, drawn and quartered! Ralph! What in the devil's armpit are you doing standing there gawping?! Go and fetch us some victuals for the night! There's a farmstead over there!'

'Come on,' whispered Alan to Tom, and the two of them turned off the muddy road towards the farmstead. 'Tell you what, Tom,' said Alan, 'I'll give you the honour.'

'How d'you mean?'

'This is one of Sir John's tenants. He has an arrangement to collect a chicken or so whenever he passes. You can be Sir John's spokesman.'

Tom shrugged. 'Whatever you like.'

'While you're doing that, I'll nip round the back and choose a nice fat one. It's got to do three of us.'

So Alan disappeared round the back of the farm, while Tom knocked on the door. The man who opened it was blinking with the smoke from his fire. He looked Tom up and down with a distinct air of hostility.

'Who are you?'

'I'm one of Sir John Hawkley's retainers,' replied Tom, feeling a surge of pride as he found himself saying the words. 'He wants one of his . . .'

'Who?' The tone of the man's voice was the first indication that this transaction was not quite as straightforward as Alan had made it sound.

'Sir John Hawkley,' whispered Tom, 'he's over there.'

The farmer peered through the rain at the bedraggled figure sitting on the wheezing horse.

'He would like one of his chickens, please . . .'

For a ghastly moment, the idea crossed Tom's mind that perhaps this was yet another of Alan's jokes and that this farmer was not one of Sir John's tenants after all and would therefore have no inclination to give him one of his precious chickens. But the man suddenly smiled and nodded.

'Wait there . . . Chicken did you say? I'll go and get one,' he said and disappeared back into the smoky interior of his cottage.

Tom turned to look at Sir John, and was just wondering what it must be like to wield such power, to be master of lands and people, and to be able to eat chicken whenever you wanted . . . when something caught him a terrific blow on the shoulder. He spun round to see the farmer swinging a flailing rod over his head.

Tom didn't wait to hear him yell: 'Chicken? I'll give you chicken! You liar! You cheat!'

By coincidence, these were exactly the same words that Tom addressed to Alan the moment he caught up with him. Alan was laughing and Sir John was humming a rather jolly tune to himself.

'That farmer could have killed me!' exclaimed Tom. 'I've got bruises all over my back. If he hadn't tripped over into that cesspit, I wouldn't have made it.'

'Oh dear! Oh dear!' grinned Alan. 'You've got a lot to learn.'

'Like never believing anything you tell me.'

'That sort of thing,' agreed Alan. It was at that moment that Tom noticed Alan had a live chicken stuffed inside his jerkin. 'And never ask for something in this game when it's much easier and creates less fuss to just take it.'

Tom was about to say: 'You mean you *stole* that chicken?', but he decided it would be a waste of breath. He was surprised, however, later that evening, when the inn-keeper had taken the chicken and boiled it for them, Sir John Hawkley seemed to eat it without any qualms. Tom wondered if he realized that Alan had stolen it.

· 17 ·

The muster at Sandwich was yet another thing that was not at all as Tom had imagined. For a start he had not been prepared for the sight that greeted them as they came over the brow of the downs outside the town. For a few moments Tom couldn't work out what he was looking at. He felt as if the world had been taken away and as if he might fall over the edge.

'Never seen the sea before?' he heard Alan's voice as his legs gave way under him and he sat down hard in the road.

The largest expanse of water with which Tom was familiar was the village duck-pond. Of course he knew the sea would be bigger than that, but he still couldn't help thinking of it as . . . well, as an extremely large duck-pond. Back in the village they had no images of such things. The only paintings were some biblical scenes on the chancel wall of their little church, which a visiting monk had painted for them many years before. Pictures and drawings were just not part of young Tom's life. So there was no way he could have been prepared for the sight that now lay before him.

But it wasn't just the sea itself that took away Tom's breath and the strength from his legs. It was the forest that bobbed up and down on the waters – the vast timberland of masts that never stood still.

'Hang me for the dog I am!' exclaimed Sir John. 'The King's got his fleet all ready to go and we've not a berth between us! If we don't look lively those villains and horse-thieves will be over the water and helping themselves to the best pickings while we're still kicking our heels in port!' And with that he kicked the sides of his horse and the poor creature wheezed and staggered off down the road as fast as its thin legs would carry it.

'Come on!' said Alan, pulling Tom to his feet. 'If we don't get on a ship tonight, Sir John'll beat us till our backsides come out of our fronts!' And the two of them raced after their master.

As soon as he entered the port of Sandwich, Tom knew he'd never been in such a dangerous place in all his life. Tom did a quick calculation. By his reckoning there must have been twice as many people on the streets as could fit into the buildings, and it didn't take a deep knowledge of arithmetic to calculate that a large proportion of them were drunk – even though it was only an hour after noon. A fight had broken out in front of the first inn they came to. Benches had been overturned and two men were shouting at each other while others held them back and a woman screamed insults at the pair of them.

Another good indication that it was a dangerous place, thought Tom, was the fact that someone had just grabbed him round the neck, dragged him backwards into a darkened alley and was now holding a very cold knife to what Tom would previously have referred to as his throat, but which now felt more like a sockful of rocks hanging from his chin.

Tom was just about to do the only thing he could think of under the circumstances – i.e. scream – when he noticed that the man was doing an odd thing in his ear. He was growling. It took Tom a few moments to realize that this growling was, in fact, a form of speech, and by the time he'd realized this he'd missed whatever it was the man with the knife to his throat had actually growled.

'I beg your pardon?' Tom managed to get out – even though his throat now felt like a vase full of thistles covered with glue.

The man growled again, and this time Tom was able to make out the odd word coming through an unfamiliar accent.

'Again?' asked Tom hopefully.

'I sayed,' growled the man with the knife to Tom's throat, 'tell your maister this: the Priest says unless he hands over what's mine he is a dead man and you are a dead boyo. I'll be at The Feathers.'

Tom was just thinking of asking for yet another encore of this impeccable growling, to give him time to think of how to escape, when he became aware that he no longer had a knife to his throat and his arms were no longer pinned to his back. In short, he no longer had anything to escape from. The man with the knife had vanished as suddenly as he had appeared. Tom's throat returned to being a throat.

Tom ran so fast out of that alley that he crashed into the first person who happened to be walking past and sent them both rolling into the gutter.

'Sorry,' gasped Tom, and he was just about to expand on this theme – explaining exactly how sorry he was – especially since most of the mud in the street now appeared to be adhering to the smart uniform of the person he'd knocked over. 'Somehow mud doesn't seem to go with black and red stripes,' thought Tom, and then he was about to repeat to himself: 'Black and red stripes!' but the words froze in his mouth. In fact Tom's

mouth kept opening and closing but not a single iced-up syllable dropped out.

'Look what you've done!' The man in the smart but now mud-caked uniform had scrambled to his feet. 'I'm filthy!' And he raised his hand to clout Tom across the ear. Now normally Tom had very quick reactions to this sort of thing, and he would have dodged out of the way long before the hand connected with any portion of his anatomy. But, in this instance, the same thing that had frozen the words in his mouth now also seemed to freeze the muscles in his legs. The result was that a violent cuff across the ears sent him sprawling back into the gutter.

Tom landed on an inert object already lying in the street, and he stifled a scream as he realized the object was a corpse. The man in the black and red livery, however, took no notice. He turned on his heel and strode off. At the same time, Tom noticed that the corpse beneath him was singing quietly to itself.

'What a bit of luck,' whispered Tom to the corpse. 'He didn't recognize me.'

The corpse now propped itself up on one elbow and looked more like a drunken sailor: 'My love has gone to a distant land,' he sang, 'Alas why has she so?'

'Probably because you stink,' said Tom.

'And I am sad, for here I stand,
And cannot near her go,'

insisted the drunken sailor.

Tom, who was familiar enough with the song not to need to hear the next verse, scrambled to his feet, and checked that the man in the livery really had gone. 'He may not have recognized me,' murmured Tom, 'but I certainly recognized *him* . . . He was one of Sir William's men, or I'm a black pudding! Can they really still be hunting for me – even here? The sooner I get on a boat to France the better!'

But before Tom could take another step, there was a commotion down the street. People started running, heads popped out of windows, and a herald in a gold-embroidered tunic came running down the street, shouting: 'Make way! Make way!' Behind him a cavalcade of horses snorted and pranced. Above them pennons fluttered and three silver-clad figures rode imperiously into town. The plumes on their helmets waved with the motion of the horses, and their coat-armour blazed with colours and emblems.

'It's the Duke of Lancaster,' murmured a voice in the crowd.

Tom withdrew into a doorway and watched. If you had looked into his face at that moment you would have sworn that there was a light somewhere inside him that was now making his eyes so bright that they almost shone in the failing light of the day.

· 18 ·

It was dusk by the time Tom finally found Sir John and Alan. They were both standing on the quay, deep in conversation with a man with no nose. Actually 'conversation' is rather a bland description of whatever it was they were deep in. Sir John was gesticulating and alternatively shouting at the man with no nose and pleading with him.

As soon as Alan spotted Tom, he pulled him to one side. 'Keep out of sight. He wants to charge us two marks *each* to get us over the Channel!'

If Tom had known as much about the coins of the realm as he did about Latin irregular verbs, he would have known that a 'mark' was worth about two-thirds of a pound. But since even a silver penny was a rare sight to Tom, all he knew was that the Man With No Nose might just as well have been asking for the moon to take them across the sea.

'What's he going to do – swim across with us on his back?' asked Tom.

Alan kicked him. 'He's captain of that ship. So for goodness' sake don't let him see you.'

The connection between his not being seen and the fact that the Man With No Nose was captain of the

85

small cog beside which they were standing was not at all obvious to Tom, but he had no time to ask for clarification because Sir John suddenly called out: 'Ralph!' And Alan jumped.

'See you at The Feathers!' whispered Alan, and ran off to join his master.

'The Feathers! Be careful! There's a man there who's threatening to kill us!' Tom knew that was what he *should* have said, but he hadn't, and now Sir John was pumping the hand of the Man With No Nose and the next minute he and Alan had disappeared.

The Man With No Nose seemed to be in no hurry to leave the quay. He stood there counting the coins in his hand and humming 'My love has gone to a distant land'. It was at that time, you see, a popular tune amongst both the living and the dead.

But Tom had no time to stop and listen – much as he liked the melody. He had to warn Sir John and Alan that the reception waiting for them at the Feathers might be livelier than they'd be expecting. Scrambling over some crates, Tom found a short cut through a back-alley into the High Street. Once there, he immediately discovered two obstacles to achieving his goal. The first was that the street was so thronged with people that he had no hope of spotting his two friends. The second was that he also couldn't see any sign of an inn called The Feathers.

'Excuse me,' Tom asked a large, brown-faced man who was carrying a large, brown-faced cake on a tray. 'Is there an inn called "The Feathers" near here?'

The large, brown-faced man beamed and Tom was almost convinced that the large, brown-faced cake beamed too. 'An inn called "The Feathers"?' he exclaimed. 'Of course there's an inn called "The Feathers"! There's always an inn called "The Feathers" – in every town – isn't there?"

'Where is it?' asked Tom.

'Ah! That you'll have to ask someone,' said the man.

'I *am* asking someone,' Tom pointed out.

'So you are,' agreed the man, and Tom noticed his face was dotted with red and black spots – exactly the same as the cake – although in the case of the man's face he doubted whether the dots were pieces of fruit. 'Stranger here myself,' said the man. 'Why not ask a local?'

Good idea, thought Tom. I wonder if locals carry large placards reading: 'Local inhabitant. Please ask directions here.' Or maybe they wear special Sandwich Local Inhabitant Hats so you can avoid wasting time asking strangers the way . . .

Tom's further thoughts on these lines were interrupted, however, by the fact that he had just turned a corner and now found himself peering down a dingy alley outside the dingiest building in which was hanging a dingy clump of blackened and bedraggled stalks of grass.

'Maybe that's not grass,' said a voice in Tom's head. 'Maybe they're *feathers*.' At which precise moment, he saw two people entering the dingy door of the dingy building. 'Stop!' cried Tom, breaking into a run. But he was too late. Sir John Hawkley and Alan or Ralph or Nigel or whatever his name was, had walked straight into The Feathers Inn.

Tom reached the dingy door of the dingy inn in about the time it would take a thirsty knight to say, 'A quart of ale, please, landlord!' or about the time it would take a dozen desperate villains to leap on two unsuspecting customers and overpower them. Tom was just pushing the door open to find out if either of these events had taken place, when he stopped himself.

'Suppose they *have* just walked into an ambush?' he pondered. 'It's not going to help them if I do the same.' So instead of walking straight in, Tom laid his ear to the door. All he could hear was shouting and cursing and banging.

'It *is* an ambush!' he exclaimed. 'I should have warned them!' And he started hopping from one foot to the other in his anxiety.

'Look,' a sterner voice in his head had taken over. 'It's no good hopping up and down like a rabbit in a pot! What is it Alan would say: "Situation . . . Alternatives . . . Action." Well, the Situation is obvious. The Alternatives are, I suppose, run away or do something. And the Action is . . . *what*? I don't know *what* I should do! But I can't run away.'

At this point, the dingy door of the dingy inn swung open as two men dragged a third out and off down the street. The man they were dragging was shouting: 'Aw! Let's get the boat tomorrow! It's early! Have another!'

Before the door swung back again Tom caught a glimpse of the dingy interior of the dingy inn. He could see Sir John and Alan sitting at a table looking remarkably unlike two people who had just been ambushed.

'Thank goodness you're all right!' said Tom as he sat down on the bench next to Alan.

'Sh!' said Alan.

'As I was saying,' said Sir John, glaring at Tom. 'There

88

were a dozen of them – evil-looking misbegotten creatures of the devil! They were lying in wait for us – miserable, sneaking cowards that they were! But *we* had crept up the other side of the ridge and it was *us* who were going to surprise . . .'

'Please, Sir John!' exclaimed Tom. 'We mustn't . . .'

'Sh!' said Alan again.

'Ahem!' said Sir John, looking daggers at Tom. 'It was *us* who were going to surprise *them*! Well, before they could so much as sneeze, our archers let fly a hail of arrows and . . .'

'But you don't understand . . .' blurted out Tom.

'Sam! It's *you* that doesn't understand . . .' Alan had pulled Tom away from the bench and pinned him in a corner against a pile of old straw. 'First thing you've got to learn is never . . . *never* . . . interrupt Sir John when he's telling one of his stories.'

Sir John was glowering at the serving-girl and drumming his fingers on the table.

'But it's not safe here!' whispered Tom. 'We all may be in danger!'

'Nothing,' repeated Alan, '*nothing* can ever justify interrupting one of Sir John's stories. It's the first rule.'

'But . . .'

Alan raised his hand. 'That's it!'

They returned to the bench and Sir John stopped drumming his fingers. 'Our archers let fly a hail of arrows. Eight of the godless scum died at once. Then we set-up a yell, charged down and cut the rest of those French pigs to pieces in the time it takes a dog to eat its dinner.'

Having said this, Sir John took a long draught of ale

and banged the empty tankard on the table. 'And another!' he roared.

'May I speak now?' asked Tom.

Nobody said 'yes' and nobody said 'no', so Tom told the story of the man who put a knife to his throat.

The effect this story had on Sir John was not at all what Tom was expecting. He did not, for example, leap to his feet, brandish his sword and bellow: 'Let the snakes come! We're ready for them – eh, Tom – er I mean Sam?' What he did was subtler than that. In fact it was so subtle you might never have noticed it: he turned very slightly white and looked at Alan.

'The Priest!' whispered Sir John.

'Why didn't you tell us?' Alan hissed at Tom.

'Well of all the . . .' began Tom.

'If the Priest comes here with some strong-arms we'll be roasted in our breeches!' said Alan.

Sir John banged his fist on the table. 'But they killed him! I saw them, Ralph!'

'Maybe,' said Alan, 'but we'd better get out of here before . . .'

At this moment, the dingy door of the dingy inn flew open, and there stood seven men of robust build – not one of whom would you ever dream of asking to do the baby-sitting.

'Golly!' thought Tom, 'tonight must be the night the Ugly Club meets!' But before he had time to add 'Pity I let my subscription lapse,' he realised that both Sir John and Alan had leapt about four feet sideways into the air, turned the table over, and disappeared up the dingy staircase that led to the no doubt equally dingy upstairs of the dingy inn.

'I didn't mean that about the Ugly Club,' said Tom aloud. 'Anyway I was only *thinking* it . . . but have any of you read the works of Aristotle, because he has some interesting things to say about Beauty and its absence . . .' And all the time, Tom was thinking: 'Why do I always blabber in situations like this? I should be using my energies to think of a way of escape. But no! Instead I'm shooting my mouth off as if it were a double-action crossbow . . .'

At which point one of the visually unprepossessing septet said 'Shut up!' – rather to Tom's relief. The seven then all stepped into the room at once, and proceeded to give it a good scowl. The room shuddered.

'The Priest's not here,' said the one with the cauliflower ear.

92

'I can see that,' growled the one with the cauliflower
nose.

'You! Get us some drink,' said the one with the
cauliflower . . . well . . . I suppose you'd have to say: the
cauliflower face.

'Yeurrchhh!' thought Tom, and then suddenly
realized that the man was talking to him. 'Yessir!'
exclaimed Tom, but, before he could move, the man had
thrust his cauliflower face right up against Tom's.

'Who was that in such a hurry just now?' asked the
cauliflower face.

'That?' Tom heard himself saying. 'Oh! That was
. . . was . . . er what was his name? . . . Sir Robert Markham
and his nephew.' Even *I'm* doing it now, thought Tom, I'm
making up people's names as if I were Alan.

'Why were they in such a hurry?' insisted Cauliflower Face.

'Why were they in such a hurry?' repeated Tom, his mind racing. 'Well . . . they were in a hurry because . . .' Tom was uncomfortably aware of the little beady eyes peering out of the cauliflower face and he found himself thinking 'Uh-oh! I'm not doing very well with this one.'

'They were in a hurry because . . . they needed to get to bed,' Tom groaned. He couldn't believe that he would have come up with such a feeble excuse.

'They needed to get to bed?' sneered Cauliflower Face.

'Well so would you,' Tom didn't know *what* was going to come out of his mouth next and was rather surprised to hear himself say: 'When you've got the Plague it's the best place to be. Besides they're not supposed to drink in public places once the sores have broken out and they were afraid you were the King's men.'

The little beady eyes in the cauliflower face blinked without expression. 'They got the Plague?'

'It's terrible!' exclaimed Tom. 'Sir Robert fought his way through Gascony with the Black Prince. Came back to England to pick up his nephew and they both go down with the Plague together!'

The man with the cauliflower face was already backing towards the dingy door, as the serving-girl came in with the ale mugs.

'You're not supposed to serve plague victims!' snarled the man with the cauliflower ear.

'We'll wait for the Priest outside,' said the man with the cauliflower nose, and they all backed out of the inn and the door banged closed behind them.

'Phew!' thought Tom. 'Thank goodness being ugly doesn't mean you're not gullible!'

'Quick thinking!' Alan's head appeared at the top of the stairs.

'But what do we do now?' whispered Tom as he joined him.

'Situation: we're trapped,' said Alan. 'Alternatives: hide or get out. Action: if we hide they'll find us – so we've got to find Sir John and get out.'

The first part was easy. They found Sir John under a bed. Getting out of the dingy inn proved slightly more problematical.

From the upstairs windows they looked down on the seven men in the street below. They had just been joined by the man who had held the knife to Tom's throat. Tom couldn't see him clearly, but he could hear the now familiar unfamiliar accent.

'You weren't swallowing a story like that now were you? You're a basketful of morons and no question!'

'It's the Priest all right!' muttered Sir John, and the trio ran into the back room upstairs that looked out on to an empty courtyard. The windows, however, were no bigger than a kennel door.

'You'll never get me through that!' grunted Sir John. He had already tried to push his shoulders out, but it was obvious there was no way he'd get his enormous belly to follow.

'We'll just have to use the back door!' whispered Alan, and the three of them were half-way down the dingy stairs when the dingy door of the dingy inn flew open once again, and the man they called the Priest burst in with his ugly henchmen at his shoulder.

Sir John froze on the stair.

'Well well well!' said the Priest. 'John Hawkley or I'm an Englishman!'

'It's you!' said Sir John.

'Full marks for stating the obvious,' thought Tom.

'Why don't we all sit down and have a friendly drink?' suggested Alan.

'I've come for what's mine,' said the Priest.

'And have it you shall,' stammered Sir John. 'I've been looking for you high and low. Been trying to get your share to you ever since we got separated . . .'

'Ever since you left me to die among those French dogs, you mean,' hissed the Priest. Tom had never heard so much hatred concentrated into so few words.

'Now that's not how it was at all . . .' Sir John was backing slowly up the staircase. The Priest and his seven bruisers were edging across the taproom.

'Whatever's going to happen,' thought Tom, 'is going to happen any minute now . . .'

'I knew you'd be able to deal with that handful of cowards,' said Sir John. His hand was now gripping his sword handle as he backed up one more step.

'So you stole my share . . .' hissed the Priest, taking another step forward.

'I was keeping it for you,' swore Sir John, taking another step back.

'It's in that bag!' cried Alan – and suddenly it happened!

The Priest sprang to the bag that Sir John had left under the table. At the same time three of the henchmen rushed for the stairs. Sir John kicked the bannister so hard it collapsed on the Priest. Meanwhile, Alan had

wrenched the hand-rail off and hurled it at the three men
coming up the stairs – so they toppled back to the floor.

The next second, Sir John had grabbed a small oil
lamp from a niche in the wall and had hurled it on to
the heap of straw in the corner. Neither Alan nor Sir
John waited to see the oil ignite and the straw burst
into flames. They had both vaulted over the side of
the staircase and had disappeared towards the back
door as fast as rats in a sewer.

One of the men, however, had picked himself up
quickly enough to follow, and Tom heard a scuffle and a

yell in the passage, before he himself raced back upstairs with two of the Ugly Club after him.

'I didn't know cauliflowers were so fast!' thought Tom as a hand caught his heel. He turned to see the man with the cauliflower face hanging on to his leg. Tom kicked with his other leg and the man let go with a cry of rage. 'That's probably how he got a cauliflower face in the first place!' muttered Tom and darted into the back room.

He hadn't got more than a leg through the tiny window, when the man with the cauliflower ear, the man with the cauliflower nose *and* the man with the cauliflower face all charged into the room.

'Whoopee!' shouted Tom. 'I've got the full set!'

The three men paused for no more than a fraction of a second, but in that time Tom had squeezed the rest of himself through the window, and found himself dropping towards a couple of figures who had just emerged from the back door immediately below.

As he hit Sir John Hawkley, Tom was already apologizing. Sir John fell heavily to the ground, his sword was knocked out of his grip and clattered across the courtyard, but his hands were already around Tom's neck and choking the life out of him.

'It's Sam!' yelled Alan, pulling Sir John off.

'Idiot!' yelled the noble knight. But there was no time for more abuse; the Priest and two of his side-kicks had appeared from the inn.

The three of them sprinted across the courtyard and through another door, slammed it in the Priest's face, and slid the great bolt across as the Priest and his men banged their fists on the wood.

The building Tom now found himself in was pitch black. It was also full of objects.

'Ow! Hell's rabbits!' yelled Sir John Hawkley, who'd just hit his toe against one of the objects.

'What was that?' said Alan as a heavy object he'd just stumbled into rolled across the floor and now sounded as if it were bouncing down some stone steps.

'I've found a door,' said Tom. 'Over here!'

At that moment there was a crashing and splintering behind them. The Priest and his men had taken a couple of axes to the door that was blocking their path.

Meanwhile Tom had felt his way along a wooden wall and discovered a large door with padlocks. 'I've got the door to the street!' he yelled. There were now shouts coming from the courtyard at the back and the attempt to break down the rear door became even more hysterical.

In the darkness Tom felt himself joined by Sir John and Alan.

'It's locked!' said Alan.

'They'll be through that door in seconds!' yelled Sir John as holes of flickering light began to appear in the door. 'Find the upstairs!'

'I've found the stairs!' cried Tom.

'Ow!' bellowed Sir John, as he banged his head against another object.

'Here!' yelled Tom and he was up the stairs with Alan and Sir John scrambling after him. 'God's bed-bugs!' Sir John was muttering. 'It smells like a brew-house in here!'

'What's that?' Alan had bumped into a large wooden object.

'Here!' called Tom. He'd found a window and in a

second he'd got the shutters open. The room was at once lit up by an orange glow.

'It *is* the brew-house!' exclaimed Alan. The object he'd bumped into was a large tun of fermenting ale, and there were sacks of malt stacked around the walls.

Sir John immediately stuck his hand into the brew and scooped up a handful of the half-fermented ale. He swallowed it down. 'I needed that!' he gasped.

Tom, however, was more engaged by what he was seeing out of the window.

'Uh-oh!' he muttered 'I think we've made our mark on Sandwich!'

The inn from which they'd just fled now no longer looked at all dingy. In fact it looked almost festive. This was because all the windows were lit up by a flickering orange light. From the downstairs doorway flames were now curling, and smoke was beginning to pour out from the upper windows.

Screams could be heard as figures ran into the courtyard. Someone appeared at one of the tiny back windows, and whether it was a tight squeeze or not they were through it and falling to the ground below.

But the courtyard was no escape. The flames had closed off the entrance from the dingy street, and the Priest and his men were still trying to break down the solid door of the brew-house.

Even as Tom watched in horror a gust of wind fanned the flames, and they licked across to catch the thatch of the one-storey dwelling next door. Tom was mesmerized by the speed at which the fire spread. But he suddenly felt himself grabbed and dragged back across the brew-house to the front room. There a nasty surprise awaited them.

'No windows!' exclaimed Alan.

'Satan's sausages!' screamed Sir John.

'Got it!' came a cry from downstairs as the Priest finally hacked through the back door.

At this point Sir John started kicking the wall. For a fraction of a second, Tom thought he was simply venting his frustration, but then he realized what Sir John was doing and joined in. By the time the Priest had mounted the stairs, Sir John, Alan and Tom had together kicked a fair-sized hole in the wattle-and-daub wall, and Sir John was squeezing out into the street below.

Alan was out next and, just as the Priest burst into the room, Tom followed. Then the three of them disappeared into the darkness.

19

Some hours later, Tom was experiencing his first sea crossing and a conflict of emotions. He was relieved to have escaped from the Priest and his Ugly Club, but he couldn't help feeling guilty as he peered across the black water at the blazing town of Sandwich.

Sir John and Alan, however, were in high spirits. 'Drink of the Devil's spittoon!' Sir John was yelling. 'We gave that Priest more than he bargained for, eh, Ralph?'

'Let's hope not even his ashes are left!' replied Alan.

'By God's gaiters! See how she's burning still!' yelled Sir John. 'The town of Sandwich is going to remember us!'

It was an hour before dawn, as their ship slipped through the forest of masts towards the open sea. There were a lot of questions Tom wanted to ask, such as: Why was their's the only ship leaving? Which was the King's ship? Where *was* the King? How long would the crossing take them? And was he really supposed to do the whole trip with a horse breathing down the back of his neck?

The horses were each boxed in by hurdles, but were still able to stamp their feet and the little boat shook continually. The reason this particular horse was breathing down Tom's neck, however, was that Tom was buried under the horse's hay. This is not how he would have chosen to travel himself, but he appeared to have no choice in the matter. And this was another reason why Tom found his first experience of a trip at sea so alarming.

Earlier, in the dead of night, he and Alan had followed Sir John to the quay, where the captain of the ship they were to sail in, a.k.a. the Man With No Nose, greeted Sir John. Alan had once again pushed Tom into the shadows: 'For goodness' sake don't let him see you!' hissed Alan.

'Why not?' Tom had managed to get out.

'I told you,' said Alan. Tom stifled the urge to say 'No you didn't' as Alan continued: 'He's trying to charge us four marks each for the crossing. Sir John's got him down to two each but all together that's still more money than we can come up with right now, so you've got to travel as baggage.'

Tom knew instinctively that 'travelling as baggage' was not a thing you'd want to do unless you *were* baggage.

'What do you mean?' whispered Tom. '"Travelling as baggage"?'

'It's quite safe,' said Alan.

'Why shouldn't it be safe?' asked Tom.

'Just don't let him see you. They tend to throw stowaways overboard.'

'Don't let him *see* me?' exclaimed Tom. The boat was no more than thirty feet long, and in lay-out looked little different from a large rowing boat. 'There's about as much chance of me not being seen as there is of Sir John not leaving any ale in his pot!' thought Tom, rather ungenerously.

'Get in here,' said Alan.

Now all the time they'd been talking, Alan had been busy taking straw out of a basket.

'I'm not crossing the sea in that!' said Tom.

'You've got no choice,' replied Alan.

'I could *not* come,' suggested Tom.

But Alan had already bundled Tom into the basket and was now covering him over with straw.

Something about being covered over with straw had a strange effect on Tom. Instead of going on arguing and struggling, he just gave up. 'It's a bit like when you throw a cloth over a bird's cage,' thought Tom, 'the bird stops singing and goes to sleep . . .' Tom yawned. The straw was warm and he suddenly realised how tired he was.

When he woke up, his basket was being manhandled up over the side of the ship. It was then thrown on to the deck without any regard to its contents.

'Ouch!' said Tom into the straw.

'Get rid of that!' Tom heard the Man With No Nose just over his head, and as he was wondering what he was referring to, he felt a sharp kick on the side of the basket. 'We've got no room for this basket – leave the straw for the horses.' Then the Man With No Nose walked away. A few moments later, Tom heard Alan's whisper.

'Tom! Are you all right?'

'For baggage I suppose I am,' replied Tom.

'You've got to get out of there without being seen.'

'That's easy,' whispered Tom. 'I've just swallowed this

pill and it's made me invisible.' There was another kick on the side of the basket. 'Ow!' said Tom.

'This is serious,' said Alan. 'When I give you the sign, get out and go and hide in the horses' hay. Understand?'

'What sign?' asked Tom. There was another kick on the side of the basket. 'Ow!' said Tom. 'Why d'you do that?'

'That's the sign,' whispered Alan.

'Couldn't you just tell me?' asked Tom. There was another kick on the basket. 'Ow!' exclaimed Tom. 'What was *that* for?'

'That's the sign!' hissed Alan urgently.

'You just told me!' said Tom.

'That's it! The Captain's not looking!'

'You mean I should get out?' There was another kick. 'Ow!'

'Get out!' Alan was already pulling the straw off Tom's head, and in another moment Tom was hiding under some hay with a horse breathing down his neck.

Now from the point of view of anyone hoping to cross the Channel in a small ship without being seen by the Captain, a horse's hay makes a reasonably good hiding-place, but it has one serious draw-back: from the horse's point of view the hay is there to be eaten. Thus the horse who was breathing down Tom's neck was also consuming his hiding-place.

Tom kept saying 'Stop it!' and 'Shoo!' to the horse, but the horse was jammed between hurdles and couldn't 'shoo!' anywhere – all he could do was go on eating the hay that was in front of him, notwithstanding the fact that it appeared to be talking back at him in a way that hay usually didn't.

'That's my jerkin!' exclaimed the hay, and it hit the horse sharply on the nose.

'Ow! That hurt!' exclaimed the horse – or at least that's probably what he meant to say, although it came out as a loud whinny.

'What's the trouble back there?' called out the Captain. 'See to the horses!' he yelled.

'Ay ay, Capt'n!' said a gruff voice, and Tom burrowed himself further down into the hay, as a sailor made his way over to the hiding-place.

'What's up, old girl?' The sailor was stroking the horse's neck. Tom could see the coarse weave of his woollen gown – he was that close. And then the worst thing that could possibly have happened happened: a piece of hay started to tickle Tom's nose.

'Oh no!' he thought. 'I mustn't sneeze! Not *now*!' He tried to remove the stalk of hay that had found its way into his nostril, but every time he moved his arm, he made a rustling noise. It probably wasn't that loud, but to Tom it sounded like a pack of rats in the thatch back home . . . home so far away that he could hardly remember it . . . hardly think of it as home . . . 'But I don't suppose it sounds like that from the outside,' Tom found the realization comforting.

'Steady, old girl,' said the kindly sailor, 'sounds like you've got a pack of rats in the thatch!' and he stabbed at the hay with his long knife. Tom went cold. The blade had missed him by inches, and any moment now he knew the sailor was going to thrust it in again.

'Ah! . . . Ah! . . . Ah! . . .' went Tom as the hay tickled his nose. 'I'm going to have to give myself up . . .'

But at that moment he heard Alan's voice: 'Hello there! I'll take care of her!'

'There's a rat in her hay,' said the sailor, and suddenly the knife stabbed into the hay again. Tom flinched as the blade skimmed the skin of his arm.

'I'll look after the horse,' repeated Alan. 'Shouldn't you look to that leak over there?'

'God's bones!' exclaimed the sailor and hurried off.

'Keep still!' whispered Alan.

'You try keeping still with someone ramming a knife at you!' exclaimed Tom.

'Sh!' whispered Alan, and the boat lurched suddenly as the offshore wind filled the sail.

'CHOO!' cried Tom at last.

But he could sneeze all he liked now, for the boat was aroar: the Man With No Nose shouted orders and seamen roared back, as the little vessel rode out of the shelter of the coast and on to the high seas.

20

Tom peered through the crack in the boards that afforded him his only glimpse of the great world outside. He could see the blazing town of Sandwich falling behind now . . . smaller and smaller. The first light of dawn was touching the wave-tops and the sea suddenly felt wider and deeper . . . deeper than anything Tom had ever imagined in his whole life.

He'd no time to be scared – not by the immensity of the sea anyway – for a shout flew across the deck like a bolt from a crossbow.

'Capt'n! She's sprung a leak!' yelled the sailor with the long knife.

'Dragon dung!' This was Sir John's voice, thick with ale, that cut through the roar of the sea and the slamming of the wind in the sails. 'You told me this was a seaworthy vessel!' Sir John had grabbed the Man With No Nose by the jerkin and was shaking him.

'Hold your noise!' replied the Man With No Nose, 'and get out of my way!' But Sir John was filled with the courage of his cups and was not about to get out of anybody's way.

'Don't you dare speak to me like that!' he cried. 'I demand my money back!'

'Demand some brains for that empty skull, you drunken sot!' The Man With No Nose clearly had no idea how to address a Knight of the Realm. 'I've got work to do!'

'This rotten sieve'll more likely send us to the bottom than get us across to France! You've cheated me of four marks! Swindler!'

'Get your filthy hands off me!' shouted the Man With No Nose.

Tom peered out from the straw. He could see Sir John struggling with the Man With No Nose. Unfortunately the increasingly violent motion of the sea was making Sir John even more unsteady on his feet than he usually was after several pints of ale, and as he raised his fist to strike him, the Man With No Nose simply pushed him and the Knight of the Realm toppled helplessly to the deck.

'As long as I'm captain of this ship and we're on the high seas, you'll do exactly as I tell you – understand?'

But Sir John was on his feet in a moment and lunging at the Captain. 'You're a louse-ridden liar! A pork-peddler! A heathen-loving Satan-snoggler!' bellowed Sir John.

'Sir John!' yelled Alan. The reason Alan yelled was, curiously enough, not that he was anxious to know what a 'Satan-snoggler' was, but that he had just witnessed the Man With No Nose do something that he considered to be a most improper thing for anyone to do to a Knight of the Realm. It was the kind of thing you might do to a villain or an imposter or a thief or a drunkard but not to a Knight of the Realm. The Man With No Nose had hit Sir John squarely on the nose – hard enough to send the Knight of the Realm staggering backwards across the deck until he tumbled over the side of the ship. At least he *would* have tumbled over the side of the ship if Tom hadn't grabbed him by the jerkin.

Now Tom, you may remember, was supposed to be travelling as baggage and he knew this was decidedly odd behaviour for the average suitcase, but he had – at the very moment Sir John was sent reeling across the deck – come to a decision. It was based on three main considerations. The first was that Sir John was going over the side of the ship only inches from where Tom was hiding. The second was that Sir John was clearly going to drown if someone didn't grab him. The third was that no one else seemed to be paying much attention to the man-overboard-to-be. There was also a fourth consideration – I'm sorry I didn't mention it before, but the fault lies in my narrative not in Tom's arithmetic. And as far as Tom was concerned it was the most important consideration of the lot: the horse had, by now, eaten most of the hay that Tom had been hiding under anyway. So, whether they threw stowaways overboard or not, Tom sprang out of his hiding-place and grabbed Sir John's jerkin.

His fingers, however, were cold and Sir John's body was heavy.

'I can't hold him!' yelled Tom. Nobody else seemed to hear him, but Alan rushed to his side.

The boat had taken on a lot of water by this time, and was listing badly. It was also being crashed and smashed as it was flung from one wave to another. Pulling Sir John back on board was rather like hauling a sack of wet potatoes out of the village pond while being juggled by a giant the size of England, thought Tom as he and Alan

111

finally heaved the Knight of the Realm back on to the deck of the *Lady Ann* (which was the name of the ship).

'Look out! Here comes the Captain!' whispered Alan, and Tom ducked behind a barrel. But the Man With No Nose clearly had more urgent things on his mind than throwing stowaways into the now raging sea.

'Turn her into the squall!' he was shouting. 'Tie them barrels down! You there! Get bailing!'

'Aye aye, Captain!' said Alan, and, as the ship tipped and span, sending Tom rattling across the deck, his friend began scooping the water out as fast as his bucket would allow.

The feeble sun, that had peered cautiously over the horizon a few minutes before, had disappeared again – as if it hadn't liked what it saw of the day and had decided to go elsewhere. It had left the morning under

the care of the biggest and blackest cloud Tom had ever
seen.

'But I bet it only seems that big and black because I'm
in the middle of the sea in a leaking ship surrounded by
waves as high as houses. I expect if I were in the old barn
back home, helping Odo sharpen coppice-stakes for a new
fence, the cloud wouldn't look nearly so menacing . . .'

At this point a bolt of lightning emerged from the
black cloud and seemed to hang between the rolling
heavens and the rolling waves for several seconds.

'I told you to reef that sail!' bawled the Man With No
Nose who had become, by this time, very much the
Captain of the Ship. 'More hands to the bailing! Batten
down those barrels!'

The clap of thunder that followed the lightning
shook the ship. To Tom the thunderclap seemed like a

voice urging the waves to leap even higher – for that's what they were doing.

'Do you know,' thought Tom to himself, 'I could almost swear that we're in the middle of a storm at sea. But then that's probably because I'm just a land-lubber with no real idea of what it's like to ride the ocean wave . . .' At that moment, one of the ocean waves in question leapt up above Tom's line of vision and smashed across the ship – sending salt-water stinging across horses, humans, barrels and bales. In a second, all the water Alan had managed to throw overboard had been thrown back with interest by the angry sea.

'Even if this *is* a storm at sea – which I very much doubt,' Tom told himself, 'it's probably nothing to these hardened sea-dogs. If it were a *real* storm at sea the waves would be three times as high and the sailors would probably all be saying their prayers.'

At which point the old sea-dog with the long knife suddenly fell on to his knees, raised his hands and eyes to the mast-top and muttered something which Tom could swear included the words 'God help us!' Whether it did or not, Tom decided for the second time that there was something more urgent for him to do than stay hidden. He grabbed another bucket, leapt to Alan's side and started bailing for all he was worth.

The sky roared and the sea howled under the boat. Spindrift flew off the heads of the waves as the crests turned over and smashed themselves against the rising water below, and the sea turned white with foam.

'Speaking strictly as a non-sailor,' Tom shouted across to Alan, 'I would say that this is *not* the ideal weather to be crossing the English Channel in!' Alan's face had gone as white as the foam, and he didn't reply. He simply redoubled his efforts at bailing-out the boat. And Tom thought that was a pretty sensible thing to do.

Sir John Hawkley had, all this time, been lying unconscious in several inches of water, rolling around as the ship tossed and bucked. It was only as a second wave smashed across the deck that Sir John began to regain his senses. Actually, regaining his 'senses' is rather a polite way of putting whatever it was Sir John had regained, for the moment his eyes opened and he had taken in that fact that they were now not only aboard a leaking vessel but caught in a violent storm, he started yelling. What it was he was yelling was not entirely clear; the whites of his eyes kept flashing and he seemed to be trying to grab at things – although all he got hold of was handfuls of foam and spray.

Suddenly there was a terrible ripping noise from over their heads. The sailors still hadn't managed to reef the sail and now the wind had caught it. The canvas tore and flew across the ship in a ragged tail.

The Captain swore and the seamen yelled and Sir John Hawkley tried to stand – his wet hair plastered across his face.

'Set me down!' he was bellowing into the wind. 'Set me down on dry land! At once! D'you hear? I demand to be set down!' But the wind didn't seem to hear him. 'The ship's sinking! We're all going to drown! Oh God! I'm sorry for everything I've done! I'll reform, I swear it! Don't let me die!' Sir John was now clutching at his squire, hampering Alan's desperate efforts to bail. 'D'you hear, Ralph? We're sinking?'

115

'That's exactly what I'm trying to stop,' muttered Alan, pushing Sir John away, as the ship lurched violently.

'Argh! That's it!' screamed Sir John. 'We're going down!' He staggered to his feet and stumbled across the deck. 'Captain!' shrieked Sir John, flinging himself on top of the Man With No Nose. 'Turn back to port! For pity's sake!'

'What the devil!' exclaimed the Captain, trying to shake Sir John off.

'I'll pay you twice what you asked if you'll just turn back to port! I can't die! Not like this! Not now!'

The Captain who had been busy stopping the leak, rose to his feet with Sir John still clutching on to him.

'Get this idiot off me!' he cried, but Sir John had him tight around the neck.

'Whatever you ask! Just set me down on dry land! Please! *Now*!' cried Sir John. 'I don't want to be here a moment longer!'

The Captain's reply consisted of one word: 'Boys!' he shouted, and before Tom had time to scoop out another two bucketfuls of water, several sailors had unceremoniously grabbed Sir John and lashed him to the mast, where he continued to yell and blubber as long as the storm lasted.

· 21 ·

The storm must have been raging for two hours when Tom heard a yell and looked up from his bailing to see what he thought was a welcome sight: land! The effect on the sailors, however, was not what he'd hoped. The land took the shape of cliffs that had suddenly loomed out of the depths of the storm and now hung above them. The sailors seemed to be pitched into a panic. Every available man, apart from the helmsman and the captain, had seized an oar and was now trying to row away from the cliffs. The roughness of the sea, however, made it a forlorn hope, and the ship was blown along the line of cliffs for some way, until the shore became flatter and more indistinct. But still the sea tore at her hull and the wind bent her mast. The water in the ship was above the horses' fetlocks, and every time the ship rolled, the water slapped against the opposite side and the ship rolled even more.

And then, suddenly – or so it seemed to Tom – everything went still. The wind no longer cut through his wet clothes. The spray no longer stung his face. The roar of the sea no longer rattled his ears. The ship no longer flung him from side to side. Tom lifted his head and his heart leapt: the wind had somehow blown them into the safety of a port.

'Yipeeee!' shouted Tom, and in his relief and excitement he threw his bucket in the air and it landed – as luck would have it – right over Sir John Hawkley's head, just as he was screaming: 'Untie me, boy! Come along there! Don't stand around doing nothing! Hey! What the d . . .'

Tom, who was the boy Sir John was addressing, was in half a mind not to take the bucket off his master's head, but it was a only brief moment of rebellion, and when he *did* take the bucket off Sir John's head he was more than amply rewarded for his good deed by the torrent of abuse that Sir John was able to invent on the spot. Tom couldn't remember all the epithets, but 'unfit for pigswill' figured rather largely, as did 'good news for the gallows-maker' and 'reject from a friar's donkey' (or perhaps it was even ruder – Tom couldn't quite hear). And when he had finished untying Sir John, he received a generous cuff around the ears for which he was particularly grateful as it warmed him up somewhat.

But before he could thank Sir John properly he felt himself grabbed from behind. The Captain (a.k.a. the Man With No Nose) had pinned Tom's arms to his side. 'You know what we do to stowaways?' he rasped.

'Yes,' said Tom, and was just about to ask Sir John for his assistance in preventing it, when a most extraordinary thing happened. Instead of finding himself hustled to the side of the ship and tossed unceremoniously overboard as he expected, Tom found his arms suddenly released, he heard the Captain give a sort of yelp and then the next moment – to his utter

118

amazement – it was the Captain himself who was suddenly flying over the side of the ship head-first into the briny sea. But the most extraordinary thing about it was that nobody had thrown him – the Captain had simply leapt off the side of the ship of his own accord.

Tom looked around at his fellow survivors from the storm. Not one of them looked relieved or even thankful. Tom couldn't understand it. Here they were, safe in harbour, having miraculously escaped from the raging seas, with a rescue boat already putting out from the quay to greet them, and yet everyone on board looked as if they'd just been invited to their own funerals.

'What's the matter with . . .' Tom was saying to Alan when the first arrow zanged past his ear and whacked into the main-mast.

'Uh-oh! We're *all* going to have to swim for it!'

exclaimed Alan, and without any more explanation he too jumped over the side – and so did everyone else – all except for the sea-dog, who was praying furiously, and Sir John. Tom's eyes returned to the boat that was heading towards them from the shore. Several more arrows thudded into the side of the ship. 'If that's a rescue boat,' thought Tom, 'I'm a Turk's dinner!'

Meanwhile, Sir John was desperately scrabbling through his baggage, looking for something. 'Of course!' thought Tom, 'Sir John won't want to miss such a chance to show his mettle – perhaps I should stay and fight alongside him.' But at that moment another arrow thudded into the hull, just below Tom's feet, and, at the same time, Tom saw Sir John pulling out not his sword but a silk surcoat, embroidered with a coat of arms.

Tom could make neither head nor tail of what was going on, so he decided to follow Alan's advice.

· 22 ·

The sea was even colder than Tom had been expecting. As he hit the water, the other thing that hit him was the recollection that he couldn't swim. Well, that's not exactly correct. The situation was more that he didn't know whether he could swim or not, since he'd never tried. The duck-pond back home was never more than a couple of feet deep, and anyway swimming in it wasn't something you did – and for good reason. In Tom's day a 'towel' was something rich people wiped their mouths with at table. Swimming was a luxury of summer days down in the river, where your only towel was the Sun. And it just so happened that where Tom lived, when the sun was warm enough for swimming, the river was never deep enough. Thus Tom did not know, at that moment when he hit that cold water in that cold harbour on the other side of the cold English Channel, whether he could or couldn't swim.

His first impression was that he could. He lashed out at the water in all directions, and found himself still with his head above the surface some moments later. The next instant, however, he couldn't see and he couldn't breathe, and his lungs were full of salty water. He burst up to the surface again, choking and spluttering. He had a momentary image of a ship and a harbour wall, and then he went under again.

'I *know* I can swim!' Tom was telling himself. 'I *can* swim!' This last remark was prompted by the fact that he had suddenly found himself staring up at the steady rain falling from the sky as he moved backwards across the water. 'Of course! This is how you swim! You just lie on your back and waggle your feet . . . Wait a minute! You don't even need to do that . . . you just lie back in the water and . . .' At this point Tom realized that he had someone's hands round his head and he was being pulled along.

He turned to try and see who it was, and immediately swallowed another lungful of cold Channel water. 'Keep still!' It was Alan shouting in his ear. 'And don't grab me! Just keep still and you'll be all right!'

Tom fought off the urge to cling round Alan's neck. He also tried to ignore the fact that it wasn't just raining rain at that precise moment. It was also raining arrows. The men he'd thought were their rescuers had already

overrun the ship and were now shooting at the crew in the water. 'Those French jackals!' Alan shouted in his ear, but then decided to save his breath, as he swam the two of them towards the shore.

When they finally reached . . . well you couldn't call it 'dry land' because the storm had saturated everything . . . when they finally crawled out of the wet sea on to the wet land, Tom promptly coughed up a bucketful of water. He then felt that if he could just sleep for ten days – just where he was – he'd be fine. But Alan was kicking him.

'Ow! Ow! Ow!' said Tom.

'Get up!' Alan was almost screaming at him. 'We can't stop here! They'll kill us!'

Tom thought about saying 'Thanks for saving my life!', but somehow the urgency in Alan's voice convinced him that he could thank him later. 'Not stopping here', however, was not at all easy. After their rough sea passage, the very stillness of the ground under Tom's feet made him feel unsteady. Then there was the question of energy. He didn't have any.

Tom looked across at his friend, and was pretty sure he was in the same state, but Alan had already dragged himself upright and was now desperately making his way across the shingle towards some wind-swept dunes.

Tom glanced behind at the ship and the armed men swarming over her decks, and then he followed after his friend as fast as he could.

· 23 ·

It was some time before Alan stopped. Tom caught up with him and crouched by his side. For some moments neither said anything.

'That's what they do,' said Alan finally.

'What?'

'They lie in wait for any ship driven in by a storm and then attack them.'

'Nice people,' said Tom.

'French!' said Alan bitterly and shut his eyes. Tom kept his open, and looked around at the dunes. It was a bleak prospect. No habitation. No creatures. Nothing much as far as he could see. And suddenly the future seemed to him about the same. Here they were, shipwrecked on a foreign shore with nothing. Nothing at all. Just the wet clothes that clung to their wet bodies and the noise of their teeth chattering in their heads.

'What'll we do?' asked Tom. He felt like one of the spikes of grass that stuck up through the sand, being blown this way and that but never getting anywhere.

'I suppose,' said Alan, making a rueful face, 'that we'd better rescue Sir John.'

'But they'll have . . . I mean won't he be . . . I mean

the ship was overrun by those men! Won't they have *murdered* him?' asked Tom.

Alan shook his head. 'Sir John'll have taken care of himself, don't you worry. He'll have probably fished out his old coat armour and convinced them he's worth a king's ransom.'

'I don't understand,' said Tom.

'In war,' replied Alan, 'if the enemy catch you alive, and if they think you're an important person – rich you know – they'll take you alive and try to get a ransom for you.'

'And what if you're not an important person and rich – you know . . . ?' asked Tom.

Alan drew his finger across his throat.

'So Sir John was getting out his surcoat with his family coat of arms on it so they'd recognize him and spare his life!' exclaimed Tom.

Alan snorted. 'Something like that,' he said, and for some reason he seemed to find it funny, 'but we'll still have to rescue him, before they find out it's all eyewash.'

'What's eyewash?' asked Tom.

Alan looked at him. 'Oh dear . . . you've got a lot to learn,' he said. As a matter of fact they both had a lot to learn. The main difference between them was that Tom knew he had.

Now, if you've ever escaped from being shipwrecked in a storm, *then* from being murdered by wreck-spoilers and *then* from drowning – all in the space of one hour – you'll know exactly how Tom felt as he stumbled out of the sand dunes and looked across that flat Flemish landscape on that October morning six hundred years ago. He was cold, wet, desperately tired and frightened. He was also lost, and not just in the sense that he didn't know where he was: he was also lost in another way. As he looked across the featureless fields of Flanders – the low dykes, the few trees – he could see no distinguishing mark that could lead him in one direction rather than another. In any direction, as far as the eye could see, the same fate awaited him. Of course, had he but known, to his left – some miles away – lay the great cities of Bruges and Ghent; straight in front of him lay Arras and Agincourt and all the uncountable wealth of Burgundy, stretching on and on, further than Tom could imagine, to the mountains and the Great Sea of his dreams. But standing there in the dripping rain on a flat Flanders skyline, it all looked the same.

'It's just how I feel inside,' thought Tom. 'I know I've

somewhere important to go, but right now I can't see what it is nor where it is I should go . . .' As he thought all this, the fields seemed to float . . . up and down like waves . . . then they started to spin and the trees whirled with them – faster and faster – and the sky became the ground and the whirling ground became the sky and everything became a summer's day in his own village and Tom was standing there staring at the ground, pulling up his stockings, while the Abbot's man talked down to him from his high horse in words no one else could understand but gradually Tom answered him in Latin:

'Yes . . . yes . . . I understand . . . I can hear you . . .'

'The good Lord preserve us!' exclaimed the Abbot's man. Tom looked up. But it wasn't the Abbot's man whose eyes met his, but a large, shabby friar, in a rough brown mantle. 'The boy speaks Latin!'

Tom found himself in a bare room. A fire smouldered in the centre. The smoke drifted up to the ceiling and meandered out of a hole in the eaves. Alan had collapsed asleep beside the fire. Tom himself was lying on a bed of straw and the friar was squatting beside him.

'Where am I?' asked Tom, again in Latin. 'How did I get here?'

'You and your friend were lying unconscious outside. It's not safe to stay here. There are rumours that the English have already landed.'

'But we're . . .' Tom was just about to say 'English' when he bit his tongue. Moments later he was glad he had.

'They are cruel, the English,' said the old man, 'and bloodthirsty. They think nothing of slaughter and torture so terrible it would be beyond the devil's imagining!'

Tom didn't know quite what to say, so he coughed and the friar gave him a drink of water.

'But how is it you can speak Latin?' asked the old man, switching to his own language. Tom's blood ran a little cold as he recognized the words as French.

'I . . . I can't speak French,' he mumbled, wondering what the friar would do when he realized he had a cruel, bloodthirsty Englishman in his care.

'And I speak no Flemish,' replied the friar. At this moment Alan stirred awake and the old man went over to the fire and peered into the iron pot that stood on it. 'And do you speak Latin too?' he asked Alan. Alan looked across at Tom.

'No . . . no . . . he doesn't,' said Tom quickly, and he signalled for Alan to keep quiet.

Tom now made one of those discoveries that is made and remade throughout the history of the world. A discovery that has been made over and over again by every living creature each and every day and yet is still the most amazing and powerful discovery – the discovery that he was hungry.

The same flash of inspiration clearly came to Alan at the same moment, for he suddenly groaned and took a deep breath. In both cases the discovery was triggered, no doubt, by the aroma of soup that the friar had released by taking the lid off the pot which was on the fire. The smell didn't so much tickle Tom's nose as grab him by the throat and start shaking him – he wasn't just 'hungry' he was, quite literally, starving.

The friar hurried over to him with the pot and started to spoon soup into his mouth. 'Go slowly,' said the

Frenchman. 'You're in a bad way.' Tom gulped the soup down. He was so hungry he hardly tasted it. He burnt his mouth but he didn't care. He was possessed by the urge to get his stomach on the outside of as much of the contents of that pot as possible.

'Hey! Leave some for me!' shouted Alan. The friar turned to look at Alan and narrowed his eyes, but he handed the pot over to him. While Alan fervently worked the spoon between the soup and his mouth, the friar spoke to Tom again in Latin. 'Where is your home?' he asked.

Tom was not normally stumped for an answer, but then again he was not one of those people who find it natural to tell lies. His mind went into a spin and he couldn't think of a single town or village in Flanders. In the end he decided to tell as near the truth as he dared. 'I haven't got one,' he mumbled. 'My parents both died in the Plague.'

The friar's face clouded, and he put his arm round the boy. 'Then we are fellow wanderers. I beg my way from place to place . . . a homeless sparrow. We must stick together you and I.'

At this moment, Alan put the pot down and looked rather shamefaced. 'Sorry,' he said, 'I finished it!'

· 25 ·

Some time later, when the begging friar had fallen asleep, Alan crept over to Tom and whispered:

'We've got to get out of here.'

'He doesn't seem too fond of the English,' agreed Tom.

'The one thing he *is* fond of,' said Alan, 'is food.' He was rummaging through the friar's knapsack and had already discovered a cheese, some bacon, and a large sausage. 'The old rascal's been stuffing it away. Well it'll do us more good than him.'

'You're not stealing it?' whispered Tom.

'Why not? He stole it in the first place.'

'How d'you know?'

'How else would he have got it?' there was a note of scorn in Alan's voice.

'He's a begging friar,' replied Tom. 'He might have begged for it.'

'You mean he got it from some poor unsuspecting widow-woman, by telling her he'd say a hundred "Hail Marys" for her soul,' said Alan. 'That's stealing, isn't it?'

'Perhaps he *will* say a hundred "Hail Marys" for her,' countered Tom.

'Have you heard him so much as whisper a prayer?' asked Alan.

Tom shook his head.

'Come on,' said Alan, 'while he's still asleep.'

'No!' said Tom, very firmly. 'He saved our lives! We can't take everything he's got from him!'

Alan rolled his eyes. 'Listen,' he hissed, 'we're in France now. This is enemy territory. We can do whatever we want.'

'I think we're in Flanders,' whispered Tom, as he tried to wrest the knapsack from Alan's grip.

'*He's* French,' said Alan pulling the knapsack back.

'But he's been good to us,' replied Tom.

At this moment a sound made both the boys freeze. It wasn't a very loud sound. It was like a slight rattle or a long drawn out scratch; it was a very insignificant sort of sound really, but both boys knew instantly what it was, and it made their hearts jump in between their ears. It was the sound of a sword being unsheathed from its scabbard. And sure enough, when they turned around, there was the begging friar, a sword in his hand, and his eyes hard and narrow in his head.

'Well, well, well, so I've caught myself a little pair of thieves,' he said, and stepped towards them.

'Tell him we surprised someone going through his knapsack and we were just checking that nothing had been stolen.' Alan hadn't even stopped to think – the story just fell out automatically. But Tom didn't have time to say a word. The blade of the sword suddenly swished, and he and Alan dropped the knapsack and leapt back.

Now compared to a machine gun or to a ground-to-air missile a sword may seem like a pretty harmless affair. But if you'd been Tom or Alan and you'd felt that blade whip past your nose, and the wind of it had blown your hair, you wouldn't have thought it was at all harmless.

The first thing to remember about swords is that they were *not* made of wood. They were made of steel. Cold steel. And they were sharp. Imagine the sharpest knife in the kitchen or a razor blade – three feet long and as heavy as a baseball bat – and you might get some idea of how dangerous a sword really was.

Tom and Alan were now flattened against the wall of the hut while the begging friar regarded them curiously.

'Nunc,' he said in broken English, 'who you?'

'My name's John and this is Philip,' Alan had started without even taking a breath. 'We came to Flanders four weeks ago with a wool merchant, Roger of Norwich, who has a regular business in Bruges. When we'd been here a few days, Philip and I decided to see a bit of the country and got lost. By the time we got back to Bruges, Roger of Norwich had sailed back and we were stranded. We've been trying to get to Calais, where we hear the King's army is mustering.'

The begging friar looked at Alan and then turned to Tom with a smile. 'And now,' he said in Latin, 'why don't *you* tell me the *real* story?'

· 26 ·

Tom felt so good to be seeing the sun rise over the flat countryside rather than having been killed during the night by an angry man of God, that he really didn't mind carrying the heavy knapsack. Alan was very subdued, but then he had his wrists tied behind his back and kept complaining that they hurt. The begging friar, however, was in a jolly mood. 'It's nothing compared to what'll hurt when they start torturing you as a spy!' he beamed, but as he said it in Latin only Tom understood, and Tom decided it wasn't worth troubling Alan with the information. 'Yes! The soldiers will be only too glad to get their hands on you, my fine lad,' continued the friar. 'You'll probably fetch me a handsome dinner tonight!'

'Tell him to speak in English,' said Alan crossly. But before Tom could say a word, the friar was clapping his hands.

'Ah! God is watching over us after all!' he exclaimed. 'Here he is sending us breakfast!'

Tom looked around but all he could see was a young farm-girl milking a cow. The friar had already waltzed over, dragging Alan with him by the rope which he had round his wrists. Tom could neither hear what was said between the friar and the milk-maid, nor could he imagine what it could be, since the friar claimed to speak no Flemish, but the net result was that God provided for them a good jugful of milk for their breakfast.

Tom had to hold it to Alan's lips, since the friar refused to untie his hands. 'Ask him where we're going and what he's planning to do with us,' muttered Alan as the friar put his head back to catch the last drops in the jug. But the friar wouldn't reply; instead he started quizzing Tom about the books he'd read in Latin.

'You must join the Church,' the friar kept saying. 'I have never come across someone so young with such a grasp of the language – you could be made for great things, young man.'

'Look,' said Tom finally, 'just let me and my friend go – *please*. We don't mean any harm . . .'

Suddenly the friar's friendly manner vanished.

'Don't mean any harm? Don't mean any harm?' he hissed. 'This villain here has come to rob and steal and kill his bloody way through my country; he and his like have already burned the villages of my childhood, they have destroyed the countryside I love – the towns, the fields, the vineyards and woods; they have murdered thousands of my countrymen; women and children have been tortured by him and his like and you tell me you don't mean any harm?'

'I'm sure Alan . . . er . . . oh I've forgotten who he said he was . . .'

'John,' said the friar coldly.

'I'm sure John's never done anything like that . . .' but even as he said this, Tom's mind went back to the town of Sandwich burning across the black sea, and the

135

laughter of his companions rang again in his ears.

They must have walked twenty miles that day. The countryside began to lose its flatness, and then in the distance they saw a town, standing on a hill.

'We're done for once we get to town,' muttered Alan through clenched teeth.

'What can we do?' whispered Tom.

'Stop whispering!' beamed the friar – he seemed to have regained his good humour.

They marched on in silence, and all the while Tom kept looking round for some way of escape. Every so often the friar would jerk on the rope round Alan's wrists and Alan would stumble. Tom caught his eye. He could see Alan's mind was working desperately too.

The closer they got to the town, the more desperate the look in Alan's eye became. Finally they began to climb the narrow road that wound up to the main gate of the walled town. The edges of the road had been cut away to form a causeway with a steep drop on both sides.

Suddenly the begging friar stopped, and turned to Tom. 'Now, my son.' He sounded quite concerned. 'Go! There is an abbey two miles down the road. Ask them to take you in. They will look after you – perhaps they will accept you into their order.'

'I can't leave him,' replied Tom. 'He's my friend.'

'Please,' said the friar. 'I know you are not a thief . . .'

'And neither is Alan!' cried Tom.

The friar was now talking rather passionately in Latin. 'Listen, I want to help you. I can see that you're meant for better things. This boy is a rogue – I know it because he's like me – we both beg our way from pillar to post, taking a little here and taking a little there, saying whatever we want anyone to believe, bluffing our way through life, but you . . . you . . . could *be* somebody . . . I can't hand you over to the soldiers to be tortured as a spy and then killed like a unwanted pup . . .'

'No,' said Tom. 'I'm not going anywhere without Alan.'

'What are you talking about?' growled Alan in English.

'Get ready,' said Tom quickly under his breath.

'Stop that!' snapped the friar, giving Alan's rope a sharp tug, and then he stared hard at Tom. 'Go! You little fool!' he said in Latin again. 'Run! I order you!'

Tom stared back at the friar for several moments, his mind racing. Finally he nodded.

'All right then,' said Tom, 'since you order me, I will. I'll join the Church and spend the rest of my life in prayer and contemplation. The abbey's two miles down the road, did you say?'

'That's right,' replied the friar.

'Very well,' said Tom. 'Goodbye, Alan.' And he turned to Alan and winked. Alan didn't move a muscle in his face. He just waited for whatever it was Tom was about to do. 'And goodbye, friar, but wait a minute! You'd better have your bag back!' And with that Tom threw the friar's heavy knapsack towards him.

The friar instinctively put both hands out to catch it, dropping the rope that was attached to Alan's wrists as he did so. But he was too late; the knapsack sailed past his ear and crashed down the steep edge of the causeway.

The friar couldn't help turning in horror to watch his bag falling with its precious contents spilling out in all directions. Neither did he have have time to yell a single curse, for Alan had already given him a sharp shove in the back, and the large, well-rounded man of religion teetered over the edge of the causeway, his arms windmilling in the air until, unable to stop himself, he followed his knapsack, half running, half rolling, down the steep slope.

Tom quickly untied Alan's hands and they both ran for their lives, down the causeway and away from town.

27

'Situation ... Alternatives ... Action!' said Alan that night as they tried to keep warm, buried together deep in a haystack.

'The situation,' said Tom, 'is that we don't know where we are or where we're going ...'

'Wrong!' replied Alan. 'The situation is that we've lost Sir John. Alternatives: find Sir John or head straight for Calais and the King's army. Action ...'

'Join up with the King's army?' asked Tom.

'Wrong again!' Alan grinned.

'But how on earth can we hope to find Sir John now?'

'Whether we *can* find him or not is another matter – the point is we've got to try.'

'Why?' asked Tom.

'Listen,' said Alan, 'you want to be a squire, don't you, Tom?'

'Very much,' replied Tom.

'First thing you have to remember is: you've got to look after your knight. He's your bread and butter. Without him you're nothing. Look at us – a couple of young beggars sleeping in a haystack. We're nothing. But as soon as we're walking behind Sir John Hawkley we're two fine young squires setting off in the King's wars.'

'All right,' said Tom, 'so what's the "Action"?'

'The "Action",' replied Alan, 'is we've got to find his trail.'

'You mean go all the way back to where we landed?' exclaimed Tom.

'Exactly,' said Alan.

Tom wanted to say: 'But it's a long way! And it's dangerous! Men there tried to kill us – that's why we ran away!' But he didn't. Alan already knew all that. They had to try and rescue Sir John Hawkley, no matter how impossible that might seem.

Actually, rescuing Sir John was to prove slightly easier than losing him in the first place.

28

It was a long weary way to walk, and the fact that they were retracing their steps made every foot seem an effort, but eventually the countryside flattened out and, after another day of hard slogging, they arrived at the outskirts of the small harbour where they had been forced to put in, and where the inhabitants had attacked them.

'Supposing he's dead?' asked Tom. 'Supposing they killed him?'

'Not Sir John!' smiled Alan. 'He'll have talked his way out of it somehow.'

'But we daren't go back in there.'

'The main thing,' said Alan, 'is to look as if we are supposed to be here.'

As he had been talking, Alan had been lifting a ladder off the side of a cottage. 'Grab the other end of this and keep walking!' he whispered. At this moment, Tom noticed a man on top of the cottage, re-thatching the roof.

'Alan . . .' he began, but Alan was walking away as fast as he could and Tom just had to follow. Even so he kept glancing over his shoulder to see when the thatcher would notice he couldn't get down, but the man was engrossed in his task, and Tom and Alan disappeared into the small town trying to look as casual as they could.

No one seemed to take much notice of them. Alan walked confidently ahead as if he knew exactly where he was going. At last he stopped outside a small inn.

'Now stand there holding this ladder and for goodness' sake look like you're waiting for me to come out again.'

'That's exactly what I will be doing,' Tom pointed out.

'I didn't want to make it too difficult for you,' replied Alan, and he disappeared into the inn.

Tom stood there for some time, humming to himself, and trying to tell himself that this was his own village, and that he recognized everyone who passed. If someone stared at him, he would nod and smile at them, and nine times out of ten they would nod and smile back.

After a while, however, Tom began to get uneasy. There was still no sign of Alan. What on earth was taking him so long? An hour or more must have passed, and Tom began to feel that every eye in the town must have been looking at him. Now he really did recognize people as they passed by for the second or third time. There was the old woman with the bent back and the black cat. She smiled at him again. Then here comes the thin man leading a calf. He didn't smile – he just looked hard and made Tom feel that he must have had 'I am English. Please shoot arrows at me!' tattooed across his forehead.

'Oh come on, Alan!' he muttered. 'Oh, there you are!' Alan had just walked out from the inn. He was looking very pleased with himself. 'What on earth took you so long?' hissed Tom, as Alan picked up the other end of the ladder and they started walking again.

'Well you can't just walk in and say: I'm looking for Sir John Hawkley, where is he? You've got to get to know them first, sit and eat and chat etc. etc.'

'Have a chat? I didn't know you spoke Flemish!' exclaimed Tom.

'I don't,' grinned Alan. 'They seem to speak quite a bit of French round here.'

'I didn't know you could speak French!' replied Tom.

'There's a lot of things about me you don't know,' said Alan. And before Tom could reply he added: 'Anyway, Sir John isn't here. He was handed over to the French.'

'Then we've lost him!'

'No, no!' said Alan. 'We've *found* him! The soldiers took him to a fortress near Saint-Quentin, and they're going to execute him in three days' time!'

'Well aren't we lucky!' exclaimed Tom.

'There they are!' A voice suddenly rang down the street. Tom looked up and saw the man who had been thatching the roof with several burly friends blocking their path.

'Who on earth?' muttered Alan.

'I think he wants his ladder back!' exclaimed Tom.

'Shall we give it to him?' shouted Alan, as the thatcher and his friends charged towards them.

'One!' said Tom.

'Two!' said Alan.

'Three!' yelled Tom, and they both threw the ladder sideways at the three men so that it landed neatly over their heads, and they fell over, entangled in the rungs and each other, shouting and cursing.

'Thank goodness my sister isn't around to hear that little lot!' grunted Tom as they ran for their lives.

'I didn't know you understood Flemish!' gasped Alan.

'I don't need to!' returned Tom, and they ran on until they came out of the town – and then they still kept on running.

That evening, as Tom and Alan made themselves as comfortable as they could in an empty chicken house, Tom said to Alan: 'We don't stand a chance of rescuing Sir John, do we?'

Alan yawned and stretched his legs, so his feet stuck out of the straw. 'One of Sir John's other mottoes is: "If it's impossible, don't think about it".'

'But that could just mean "don't think about doing the impossible",' Tom pointed out.

'Today I think it means we shouldn't think too hard about something that seems impossible, because maybe it is and maybe it isn't, it all depends . . .'

'Depends on what?' asked Tom, but already his eyes were closing.

'Depends on, depends on . . .' Alan discovered he was asleep before he could finish his sentence, but as he was asleep he didn't realize it. And, in any case, Tom was asleep before he could hear what it was that Alan didn't say. So all in all they understood each other perfectly.

29

Rain on the roof of a chicken house makes a
pleasant, reassuring sound, like far-off hoof-
beats – or at least that's what young Tom
thought to himself as he woke up the next morning. He
looked across at Alan to discover his friend wasn't lying
with his feet sticking out of the straw. In fact he wasn't
there at all.

Tom crawled out of the chicken house to make another
discovery. It wasn't raining. The sound of distant hoof-
beats was actually the sound of distant hoof-beats. Alan
was up a nearby tree, peering into the distance.

'They're heading this way!' he shouted.

'Who are?'

'I expect we're about to find out!'

Tom wanted to say: 'Wouldn't it be wise to hide –
because if they're Frenchmen they won't think twice
about killing a couple of young English ragamuffins like
us, and . . .' But he didn't say any of this, because the
band of armed men had already ridden up, and Alan was
already standing in their path and yelling at them.

There were about thirty armed men on horseback. At
their head was a knight wearing an emblazoned surcoat
of gold, blue and red. Around him rode a dozen men in

similar colours, and at his side a squire, wearing velvet and silk, was carrying his helmet. The group came to a halt, and Alan spoke quickly and urgently. There was a murmur of interest from the group, and finally the knight nodded to Alan, whereupon Alan jumped up behind one of the men-at-arms, grinned down at Tom and nodded his head, as if to say: 'Jump on the next horse!'

Tom had enough presence of mind not to ask all the questions that jumped into his head such as: 'Aren't they going to kill us?' and 'They're Frenchmen, aren't they?' Under the circumstances he decided his curiosity could wait, so he allowed himself to be lifted up on to the next retainer's horse and off the party galloped.

The thunder of the horses' hooves filled Tom's ears and drowned out whatever it was the man to whom he was clinging said. Then the hoof-beats died away, the heavens opened and the rain came down like a hail of arrows, and Tom realized that the thunder of the horses' hooves was, this time, actually thunder. It was clearly a day for mis-interpreting sounds.

The water from the sky slid off Tom's hair and ran down his back and front, down his legs and feet. The water from the horse's sides sprayed up every time the horses' legs hit the ground, and the water from the man's helmet runnelled off the rim and poured straight on to Tom's head like the gutter-spout on a cathedral.

'I suppose this is what a water-butt feels like,' thought Tom, and he buried his head in the man's jerkin, that smelt of wet leather and madder dye.

In this way the party splashed and crashed across the countryside, which became more hilly and wooded. The

man tried to shout something at Tom a couple of more times and then gave up the effort. And Tom decided not to say anything. He just kept his head down and clung on as best he could.

Some time later, they came to a halt at a deserted village. Every house, barn and shed was empty. Doors and shutters hung open, swinging in the wind, and the rain poured through the threadbare thatches on to the bare earth inside. Everywhere looked forlorn and lifeless. Nevertheless, the men set about building a fire and pulled out provisions to make a meal.

Alan pulled Tom to one side and whispered: 'You'll never guess what this swine of a Frenchman's name is!'

'What?'

'Sir Galahad!'

'Sir Galahad!' exclaimed Tom.

Alan grinned – he could see Tom was really excited for a moment, as images of King Arthur, Guinevere, Excalibur, Sir Launcelot and all the Knights of the Round Table lit up the ruined cottage. 'Sir Galahad de Ribemont,' Alan almost spat the words out. 'A French imposter! I told him we'd escaped from a gang of Englishmen from the Duke of Lancaster's army and that they were hiding out in these woods somewhere.'

'But what are we doing now?' whispered Tom.

'We're showing them where the Englishmen are.' Alan was whispering this last bit hurriedly as the French knight was approaching them.

'What? We don't even know where . . .' But Tom couldn't say any more, because the Frenchman was speaking to Alan.

Sir Galahad de Ribemont's coat armour was soaking

wet and had lost some of its shape, but the colours were vivid and the gold thread shone even on that sodden wintry day. His black beard was neatly trimmed and his manner was courtly and soft.

Suddenly he turned on Tom, and spoke gravely in English to him. 'So you are English?'

For the moment Tom thought: 'I've been betrayed! Alan's given me away to save his own skin!' But Alan was winking at him behind Sir Galahad's shoulder. 'I was telling Sir Galahad about how you were being mistreated,' he said, 'and how you helped me escape from your cruel masters.'

'Ah!' said Sir Galahad. 'There is no cruelty nor any treachery the English will not stoop to. Look at this poor land you see around you. Already it has been wasted in the wars, the farmers have abandoned their homes and fields, and now your King is on his way yet again to bring terror and death to this land.'

Tom fumbled around for a few words, but couldn't find any.

'You see the country starving – there is no hay in the barns, no animals in the farmyards, the fields are unsown, the orchards broken down and the buildings scorched and ruined. The poor country people seek shelter in the towns, but there is little enough to feed them on there, and little enough safety if the English should choose to attack. It is said King Edward has brought the biggest army ever seen in battle to these shores?'

'So they say,' Tom managed to stutter.

'We are on our way to the fortress of Peronne, where they have no one to defend them. You are welcome to come with us.'

'Thank you,' said Tom. And that was how Tom found himself in the retinue of a French knight riding out against the English. It didn't seem at all right, when he thought about it, but on the other hand, it didn't seem quite as wrong as it might have done.

30

'So where are these Englishmen of yours hiding, Robin?' Tom was not at all surprised to find Sir Galahad was addressing Alan.

'They were in the woods beyond the next village,' replied Alan without batting an eyelid. 'Of course, they may have moved on.'

'Let's hope not!' exclaimed Sir Galahad. 'I want to teach these English curs a lesson!'

When they reached the next village they found it was still inhabited. The villagers had constructed a wooden wall around the church. They had blocked up the windows and strengthened the doors, and had positioned arrows, spears and heavy rocks in the church tower.

Sir Galahad strode round their precautions, while the poor villagers waited anxiously for his opinion. 'Tut-tut! This'll never do!' he kept muttering. 'They'll soon have that door off its hinges! Where are the oil cauldrons? How will you heat them? How will you get them up to the tower? How many men can shoot?'

Finally he gathered the villagers round. 'Now listen,' he said. 'A few men may be able to hold out here for a couple days, but it's not going to be much good if the main army attacks, and the English aren't far off. My advice is to send your women and children with us – to the fortress at Peronne. Just leave a handful of men here to guard your possessions in the fortified church.'

There was a general nodding of heads. Then Sir Galahad turned to Alan. 'Robin!' he called out. 'Take your friend Robert and scour the woods ahead to see how many English are still here. You can take a couple of horses.'

'Can you believe it?' whispered Alan, as he and Tom swung themselves up on to a couple of disappointingly small horses. 'These French dolts have given us everything we need to rescue Sir John! I thought we'd have to steal the horses – I never imagined they'd hand them to us just like that! We'd never have made it in time on foot! Saint-Quentin here we come!' And, laughing, he spurred his horse towards the woodland beyond the village.

Tom followed with mixed feelings.

They hadn't ridden far into the wood when Alan turned his horse's head and said: 'This is far enough! We can head for the high road now . . .' But even as the words were leaving his lips, Tom hissed 'Sh!' and reined his horse to a halt. Alan followed suit and the two of them stood there listening intently. A horse whinnied a few hundred yards away. And now they could hear voices and the clatter of arms and armour – a body of men was making its way through the wood.

'They're speaking English!' exclaimed Tom, and the two friends pressed forward through the rather dense section of wood that separated them. After a few yards they found themselves on the edge of a clearing where a group of horsemen were standing still, listening intently.

'There's only a dozen or so of them,' muttered Alan, 'we'd better warn them about Sir Galahad and his Knights of the Square Table!' Tom grinned at Alan, and Alan cupped his hand to his mouth. 'Hey!' he shouted. 'Who's there?'

The men in the clearing peered into the trees and undergrowth and stood up in their stirrups to get a view of the new-comers. Then the leader, a knight wearing black and green coat armour, emblazoned with a bull's head, called out in a guttural tone.

Tom looked at Alan, and Alan looked at Tom. 'That's not English!' they both said at once. Alan took another look at the knight. 'I think he's German!' he whispered. 'Quite a few of Germans have joined the Duke of Lancaster.'

'So he's on our side?' asked Tom nervously.

Alan shrugged and shouted back: 'Do you speak English?'

The knight of the bull's head replied again in German.

'Try French,' suggested Tom. The moment he made this suggestion, Tom knew it was a mistake, but the words had left his mouth, Alan had nodded and shouted back at the knight in French. It all seemed to happen in slow-motion. The words drifted slowly across the glade – the knight turned slowly to his companions – the companions slowly raised their arms and several slowly pulled out crossbows while others slowly drew swords and Tom could see – still in slow motion – the heels of their feet slowly digging into the sides of their horses all as if it were happening very far away and in another world.

Then a crossbow bolt suddenly thudded at real speed into the tree just behind Tom's ear.

'THEY *CAN* SPEAK FRENCH!' yelled Alan. 'THEY THINK *WE'RE* FRENCH! RUN FOR IT!'

It seemed so obvious, now, that if the German knights could understand French they might well assume that whoever was addressing them in French *was* French, but now it was too late; the Germans were spurring their horses across the glade towards the two Englishmen.

Alan turned his horse right round, dug his heels in and Tom followed suit. Before the next bolt whizzed over their heads and thwacked into a nearby oak, they were plunging and crashing through the wood, with the Germans in pursuit.

And now Tom no longer felt disappointed at the size of his horse, for a small mount was a positive advantage as they dashed under low branches and smashed between bushes. Their pursuers, on their great war-

horses, found the boughs of trees stopping their path
time and again, and although the great beasts crunched
through most of the undergrowth, there were other
times when they were forced to make a detour, and Tom
and Alan gained ground until they finally burst out of
the wood well ahead of their pursuers.

'What's the French for "We're on your side!"?' asked
Tom breathlessly, as they thundered across a stretch of
common land towards the village.

'I don't think it matters much,' shouted Alan and he
nodded ahead of them. Sir Galahad de Ribemont and his
followers had disappeared from the village green where
they had been assembled, though the significance of this
quite escaped Tom for the moment.

The events that followed seemed to happen with the
remorseless inevitability of one of those ancient tragedies
that Tom had read with the village priest, back home in
an England that seemed further away than a mouse hole

does to a mouse that finds itself staring into the face of a cat.

As Tom and Alan reached the first cottage in the village, the German knight and his small band broke out of the wood and headed up the hill towards them. By the time Alan and Tom had reached the village green, their pursuers had gained ground and were closing in on their kill.

However, by this time, Tom had realized where Sir Galahad and his men had disappeared to. In another moment so did the German knight and his men, for with a sudden whoop and an ear-splitting series of shrieks, the Frenchmen suddenly burst out from behind the barns and cottages where they'd been hiding and descended on the Germans.

Tom had never seen anyone killed before, and he was quite certain he never wanted to see it again. It happened quite quickly – almost casually. The Germans suddenly looked round them with blank faces, and realized they'd ridden straight into a trap. They were twelve against fifty. Before their leader could bellow a curse, he was struck simultaneously from behind and in front and from the side by five or six Frenchmen. The swords clashed into each other through his flesh and his body seemed to burst apart as it fell into the mud.

Tom turned away, sick in his stomach, but he heard the shrieks that came from the rest of the band, and he knew when he turned back they would be all lying in mangled heaps under their horses' hooves.

Alan had put his arm round Tom. 'Uh-oh!' he whispered under his breath, 'not quite what we intended.'

'We led them into the trap,' whispered Tom. 'They were on our side!'

But Alan shrugged. 'War doesn't make sense.'

The next moment they found themselves confronted by a jubilant Sir Galahad de Ribemont. Tom thought he'd never seen anyone quite so pleased with themself in all his life. There was a streak of blood across Sir Galahad's tunic and he was breathing hard.

'Well done!' he exclaimed. 'You did exactly the right thing! You led them right into our hands! Perfect!' and he shook both Alan and Tom vigorously by the hand.

'Damn!' said Alan, when Sir Galahad had moved on to shake someone else's hand equally vigorously. 'We ought to have been half-way to Saint-Quentin by now! Sir John's going to be dead by the time we reach him! And a dead knight's no use to us – no more than those poor men lying out there.'

Tom just sat there. He felt gloomier than he ever had done. Partly he felt gloomy about their chances of rescuing Sir John from execution in whatever fortress he was now imprisoned. Partly he felt gloomy about leading the German party to their deaths – albeit unwittingly. But then there was something else that made him even gloomier – something that he could not quite put his finger on – but something that he knew was deep inside him . . .

31

The next day they travelled for hour after hour over the high plains of Picardy, where the land seems to come up to your chin and the world of men – farms and churches, fields and hedgerows – is compressed into a thin line between the vast sky and the vast earth. Tom felt like a tiny ant held up on the palm of the world's hand for inspection by God . . . and it made him uneasy, as if the events of the previous day had somehow been his fault.

Alan was also a little subdued but whenever he caught Tom's eye, he'd brighten up and wink and say: 'Don't worry! We'll slip away tonight!' or 'We'll take our chance before we reach Peronne.'

But the rose-red walls of Peronne came into sight, and still Tom and Alan were riding their small horses in the retinue of Sir Galahad de Ribemont. The fifty men-at-arms clattered and chattered around them, while the fugitive villagers walked or half-ran at their heels, trying to keep up with the horses, struggling to carry their possessions and pausing only to encourage their children and animals.

A moat ran round the walls and a causeway led up to the main gate. Tom's heart sank. It was a strongly fortified town, and he could see no possibility of escaping once they were inside – certainly not in time to rescue Sir John from his fate.

'We still don't even know how far it is to Saint-Quentin!' he complained to Alan as they stood outside the town walls, waiting for the gatekeeper to check Sir Galahad's letters of assignment. For certainly, in such troubled times, no town would allow a party of fifty armed men inside its walls unless they knew very well who they were.

In this case there seemed to be some sort of argument going on, and Tom could hear Sir Galahad getting annoyed – even though he didn't understand what was being said and even though Sir Galahad was trying to keep his temper.

'Well, from what I understand, we're not that far from Saint-Quentin now,' said Alan. 'It's just a question of getting away from this lot, getting out of the city, and then . . . well . . . finding Sir John . . . and then . . . er . . . rescuing him . . .' Even Alan's cheery voice had lost its conviction by the end of this sentence.

'But when are they going to execute him?' Tom secretly felt the whole thing was now so impossible that it would be better to face up to the fact. Alan, however, would have none of it.

'Probably by tomorrow noon,' he said. Tom gave a snort. It *was* impossible. And then Alan added: 'That is, provided they don't decide to execute him tonight.'

At this moment there was a whoop and a rattling of spears on shields from the soldiers as the gates of Peronne were finally lifted. Sir Galahad had completed the formalities with the gatekeeper and now they all filed into the city. All, that is, apart from the pathetic straggle of villagers. They stood there dumb-mouthed and helpless as the gates closed behind the soldiers, excluding them from the safety of the city walls.

Tom had been looking round for any way of escape – any way he and Alan could avoid entering the town and being trapped overnight, but he could see none. Now as he passed under the portcullis and the heavy iron grill crashed down behind him, he looked back in surprise at the women and men standing there, clutching their children and belongings, with their animals scattered amongst them – every one of them defenceless and exposed to marauders and weather and whatever else the night might bring.

'It's shameful! You invite us here to protect you, and yet when we bring these poor people to share in that protection you won't let them in!' Tom didn't really need Alan to translate what Sir Galahad de Ribemont was saying to the Mayor of Peronne – he could follow it all from the tone of voice. He could even take a guess at the Mayor's reply.

'Sir Galahad de Ribemont, the city of Peronne welcomes you and your men with open arms.' Here the Mayor bowed. 'We thank you for coming to our aid in these dark times. But we made no contract with you to bring extra mouths to feed into the city. Our supplies are barely sufficient for ourselves – let alone you and your men. There is simply not enough food in the city to provide for these country people who have followed you.'

'They are under my protection,' countered Sir Galahad. 'I have given them my word.'

'*We* have made no such undertaking.' The Mayor smiled at Sir Galahad and appeared to think the conversation was at an end. He was standing on the steps of the imposing Town Hall that was built of stone and was evidently still under construction. The Mayor's family were grouped around him – his wife, wearing a yellow coat trimmed with grey fur, and four rather well-fed children. A crowd of townsfolk had turned out to see the arrival of their defence force, and now a cheer went up as the Mayor signalled for the drums and trumpets to start. He pointed for everyone to look up at the top of the Town Hall where a flag was promptly unfurled.

The fact that it was the flag of Sir Galahad de Ribemont seemed to mean nothing to Sir Galahad, for he had ridden up to the musicians and silenced them. The Mayor span round as Sir Galahad rode his horse up

the stone steps of the Town Hall and lifted first one of the Mayor's children and then another up on to his saddle. He then rode down again and turned his horse round to face the Mayor.

'Since the city is so short of food,' called out Sir Galahad, 'these two little fat sparrows had better not eat anything until all the people under my protection are safely in the city!' Then he turned his horse around and led his men off through the silent crowd. The two fat sparrows chirruped as they were carried off, but the Mayor scowled and his wife turned the colour of the fur on her coat.

So it was that before night fell, preparations were once again made to raise the gates of the city of Peronne. The villagers who had sought the protection of Sir Galahad de Ribemont, clustered at the portcullis, pleading with the gatekeeper and shouting the name of de Ribemont. Some clutched on to the iron bars with both hands, others thrust their heads and arms through, while others had actually climbed up on to the portcullis and were shouting at the townsfolk within. The gatekeeper, who had been instructed to raise the portcullis and open the gates again, was trying to get them off the iron grille so that he could raise it. But nobody was listening to anybody else, and as fast as he was able to persuade one lot to let go of the gate and stand back, another lot rushed forward.

Tom and Alan were watching this pantomime with their hearts in their mouths. They had managed to get away from the rest of Sir Galahad's men and to keep hold of their horses. At this moment they were sitting astride them in the shadow of a derelict smithy that stood opposite the main gate.

'Don't wait for the people to get out of the way,' warned Alan. 'As soon as the portcullis goes up, ride as hard as you can for the gate. They'll get out of the way quick enough.'

'It's not much of a plan,' muttered Tom.

'You got a better one, Master-mind?' asked Alan.

Tom concentrated on keeping his mount still. 'We'll never get to Saint-Quentin before dark. It'll be another night in a hedgerow,' he grumbled.

'Look!' Alan sounded exasperated. 'If you'd rather stay here, and let Sir John be executed, then fine. Do that. Stay in this French fop's service, and see what King Edward and his army do to you when they storm this place in a few days time!'

The gatekeeper had by now managed to beat off most of the villagers, and had decided that the best way to communicate what he intended to do was actually to start lifting the portcullis. The moment he began to do

164

this, the men who had climbed on to it had to jump for their lives. The villagers went quiet for the moment, as they realized what was happening. But then the portcullis stopped – it seemed to have jammed.

In the shadow of the smithy, Tom and Alan gripped their reins. Their horses sensed their excitement and stamped their feet.

'Here we go,' said Alan. 'Wait for it . . .'

But now more of the villagers had come running forward and, once again, many of them tried to storm the portcullis and the gatekeeper was hitting them with a broom-handle and screaming: 'I'm trying to raise it! Dolts and imbeciles! Get off! I'm letting you in!'

As this was going on, Tom heard another noise coming from the direction of the main square: cheering and laughter and the sound of a great throng of people.

'What's going on *there* I wonder?' he muttered.

'Damn!' exclaimed Alan. The gatekeeper had now lost his temper completely. He had lowered the portcullis again and was refusing to raise it until all the villagers got off it and stood back. The villagers, however, were too excited to hear what he was yelling at them. 'This'll go on all night!' moaned Alan.

'Then I'm just going to see what's going on in the town square,' whispered Tom, and before Alan could hiss, 'There's no time! You're crazy! I'll go without you!' Tom had spurred his horse out of the smithy and down the street towards the sound of the crowd.

Tom couldn't explain afterwards why he did this. It seemed pretty illogical – there he was waiting for his moment to escape and the next minute he was riding into the town square to see what all the fuss was about.

It was one of those pointless things that Tom sometimes found himself doing – and yet he couldn't help it. It was as if some small part of his brain told his body to do the exact opposite of what most of his brain thought he ought to do. And the small part always seemed to win.

He rounded a corner in time to see a large crowd surge into the square. People were shouting, cat-calling and laughing and clearly having the best time since last Carnival! The next minute Tom had whirled his horse round and was riding hell for leather back to the gate. He arrived just as the gatekeeper had finally persuaded the villagers to stand back and the portcullis was just going up. Before Tom could reach the stable, there was a cry and the pounding of hooves as Alan charged for the gate. The portcullis was not even half-way up.

Tom dug his heels into his horse and urged it on. 'Alan!' he was screaming. 'Wait!' But Alan was screaming himself and couldn't hear a thing, as he plunged under the portcullis, swinging his body low and away from the horse as he did so. Tom followed suit as the villagers scattered out of their way and the gatekeeper yelled after them.

By the time Tom caught up with Alan, they had crossed the causeway to the other side of the moat and the portcullis was almost fully up.

'We did it!' yelled Alan.

'TURN ROUND!' yelled Tom. 'WE'VE GOT TO GO BACK!'

32

Tom didn't wait for a reply. He grabbed Alan's reins and jerked the horse round so that they were galloping back across the moat towards the main gate of the city of Peronne. By this time, the portcullis had started its descent, and both boys knew that it came down considerably faster than it went up. They also knew that if it landed on top of them, it would crack their heads open like eggs on an Easter morning. Tom screamed and Alan screamed as the metal grille gathered speed, but it was too late to stop their horses now! They just had to go for it, and that is what they did.

Any mathematician worth his salt, who had measured the distance between the two boys and the city gate, who knew the velocity of the portcullis's descent, and who could accurately ascertain the speed of the boys' horses, would have told them not to do it. A half-way decent geometrician would have informed them that they would undoubtedly end sunny-side-up beneath the city gate. Both experts, however, would have been wrong. For no mathematician can take into account the accidents of Fate.

The gatekeeper had been in a bad mood even before he had been instructed to let the fugitive villagers in, for he had been experiencing problems with his chain mechanism. The links had somehow developed a twist and tended to jam whenever he tried to raise the portcullis. That is what had happened moments before, when the villagers were clambering on it. This time, however, it jammed on the way down. It hadn't done this before, and the gatekeeper knew it meant he would have to spend precious hours (when he could have been in the ale-house) fixing it. The only fact relevant to this story, however, is that the mechanism jammed at the very moment that Tom and Alan swooped, screaming underneath the portcullis. The heavy iron grille thus stopped an inch above their backs. Neither of them ever realized how lucky they had been.

The only person who did was the gatekeeper, and he leapt out of his porch and screamed as well: 'You good-for-nothing rapscallions! What the devil d'you think you're playing at! In and out like jack-in-the-boxes!'

And the poor villagers also screamed for good measure, as they once again scattered in front of the boys' horses.

'Sorry!' yelled Tom, and he and Alan disappeared down the street towards the market-place.

'Tom!' shouted Alan. 'What are we doing?'

'Look!' Tom shouted back by way of explanation.

It didn't seem much of an explanation, but Alan looked anyway. He looked and he saw a crowd of very merry people milling about the town square. He saw a lot of merry housewives. He saw a lot of merry husbands and merry tradesmen. He saw some merry soldiers. Finally he saw a figure at the centre of all the commotion who was not at all merry. It was, however, a

169

figure that Alan recognized instantly, even though he had never before seen him sitting backwards on a donkey and wearing a chamber-pot on his head.

'Sir John!' Alan exclaimed. 'What idiots we are! We knew Peronne was a fortress. We knew it was near Saint-Quentin. And yet we were trying to escape from it!'

'And look over there!' added Tom.

Alan looked towards the other side of the square where a wooden scaffold had been erected. On it stood a man with an axe, a priest, and a chopping block. Alan gave a long low whistle. 'Not a moment too soon!'

As far as Tom could see it was more like 'a moment *too late*'! Sir John Hawkley now reached the scaffold, and the merriment of the crowd reached fever pitch. Sir John was wearing a fine surcoat, embroidered in blue with the fleur-de-lys, which set off the delicate brown glaze of the chamber-pot on his head. He was certainly not enjoying his execution as much as the crowd, however, and he kept scowling at everyone. The donkey's tail kept flicking up into his face and he nearly fell off every time someone in the crowd poked or prodded him, for his hands were tied firmly behind his back.

Tom felt his cheeks burning with shame and indignation for the great man, as he and Alan quickly dismounted and tied their horses up in the side-street. Then they slipped in amongst the crowd.

Tom suddenly felt Alan tugging his sleeve. 'Here's the knife,' said Alan.

'What knife?' asked Tom.

'*The* knife!' insisted Alan, slipping an object answering to that description into Tom's hand. 'You

170

stick close to Sir John – make sure he sees you. I'll cause a diversion. The moment everyone turns, cut his hands free and and throw this over his head.' Alan thrust a cloak into Tom's hands. 'Meet you at the old smithy.'

'Where did you get that from?' asked Tom looking at the fine woollen cloak he was now holding.

'Don't stop to think – just cut him free the moment the diversion happens,' replied Alan, as he turned away.

'Alan!' hissed Tom. 'What are you going to do?' But Alan had disappeared into the crowd.

Tom took a firm grip on the knife and on the cloak and said to himself: 'I suppose this is what you would call an "adventure" if you weren't in the middle of it.' The truth is that to Tom it felt more like a nightmare – one of those dreams in which you don't quite know what is going on and everyone else does, and yet you know one false move on your part and the whole thing will turn frighteningly nasty.

Tom also wished he could understand what everyone was shouting, because it was evidently extremely funny. Nevertheless he pushed his way through the crowd once more, until he had Sir John in his sight. A large man with a large nose had just emptied a large jug of water over Sir John, and this had produced a large squeal of delight from the gathering.

'I guess their sense of humour is too subtle for me,' muttered Tom – at which moment, the noble knight caught sight of him and scowled even more than he was scowling already. Tom tried to adopt an expression that would communicate something encouraging on the lines of: 'Hang on, Sir John! Rescue is at hand!' but he was afraid his manner was actually communicating something more like: 'Help! What am I doing? I'm going to get smashed to pieces by this mob as soon as I try and help you, Sir John!' – because that is certainly what Tom was feeling.

At that moment a surge in the crowd pushed Tom up against the back end of the donkey and into close proximity to Sir John himself. Tom took the opportunity to hiss in Sir John's ear: 'It's me! Tom . . . I mean . . .' For a moment Tom couldn't remember what name Sir John knew him by. 'Er . . . Sam!'

'What the devil d'you think you're . . .' Sir John was *not* in one of his happiest moods, but before he could complete his sentence, a most sensational thing happened to the crowd. Everyone suddenly stopped laughing. Their faces dropped – chins practically hit the ground at their feet – and then every single one of them turned to look towards the church end of the market square.

'Pity Alan's not here!' thought Tom. 'This is exactly the sort of diversion he wants to create!' A fraction of a second later (and Tom had no idea why it took him so long) the thought occurred to him that perhaps this *was* the diversion and that Alan had just created it. But how?

'It doesn't matter *how* he's done it!' Tom told himself, 'I've got to do my bit – *right now*!' And yet he found he couldn't move.

'Come on!' he yelled silently at himself. 'You haven't got time to work out how Alan's done it! You've got to cut Sir John free while everyone's attention is distracted and throw the cloak over his head! Quick, Tom!' But it was as if his mind had grown roots that went down through his body and legs, down through his feet and down into the hard, deep ground of the market square, and that wouldn't let him move until he understood what was going on. It all occupied less than a split second, but as far as Tom was concerned it seemed like an hour.

Then suddenly he heard it – ringing out over the town: CLANGA-CLANGA-CLANGA. The church bell! It was so obvious! Of course that's what Alan had done! He was up there in the church tower ringing the bell for all he was worth! For in those troubled times, the church bell wasn't used for summoning people to Sunday service – circumstances were too dangerous for that. The church bell was kept silent from year-end to year-end – and was reserved for warning of an enemy attack.

There were many townsfolk who had forgotten the very sound of the church bell. There were young children who had never heard it at all. CLANGA-CLANGA-CLANGA. But there it was now, and its sound froze the marrow in their bones.

The moment Tom realized all this, it was as if a spell had been lifted, he cut Sir John's hands free and the next second Sir John had swung himself off the donkey and Tom had thrown the cloak over his head. By the time anyone in the crowd turned their attention back to the now riderless donkey, Sir John Hawkley and Tom had vanished into the throng.

33

Tom was, quite frankly, astonished. He was more than astonished – he was gob-smacked, and his gob-smackedness was caused by several things. In the first place he couldn't believe that he and Alan had actually achieved the impossible. Not only had they found Sir John Hawkley, they had even rescued him from execution as well. But the thing that *really* gob-smacked Tom with a gobsmackeringness that was right off the top of the scale of Global Gob-smacking Championship Performances, was the fact that Sir John showed not the slightest trace of gratitude.

'Where the hell have you two good-for-nothings been?' he was growling, as they hurried through the darkening streets. 'I could have been dog-meat by now!'

'I'm sorry, Sir John!' Tom was actually thinking: What am I doing – apologizing to this man for rescuing him? But he said: 'We found you as quickly as we could! Here's the smithy!'

They ducked into the darkness of the derelict smithy, and Sir John stamped around, cursing under his breath and occasionally hitting things with his fist. And Tom found a strange thing happening – he began to feel sorry for Sir John Hawkley – the great Knight of the Realm of

England, for Tom suddenly realized that beneath the great man's anger he was scared. Sir John had been in mortal fear of death, and whereas on the boat the same fear had turned him into a quivering jelly, here it had made him fighting mad.

Some time passed, and the darkness of the derelict smithy deepened as night closed in around them. Sir John had stopped stamping around and was now sitting in a corner, staring into space.

For some time they heard the cries and shouts of a man-hunt, but with darkness the townsfolk seemed to lose their interest in the evening's entertainment, and one by one they had returned to their own hearths to eat and drink and remember the scowling face of the Englishman they would kill tomorrow when they could get hold of him.

'Where's Alan?' Tom found himself speaking aloud.

'Who?' snapped the knight.

'Ralph,' Tom corrected himself. 'He said he'd meet us here.'

'Probably in the tavern, if I know that rapscallion!' Sir John was hungry – Tom could tell by the rumbling of his temper. 'Why don't we have any meat with us?' he said. 'I'm as empty as the Pope's plate on a Friday!'

Tom was pretty certain that the Pope didn't actually fast on a Friday, but he knew better than to question Sir John's figures of speech. Tom was also pretty certain that something had gone desperately wrong for Alan, otherwise he would have been there with them.

Tom was absolutely right.

· 34 ·

The coming of morning did not improve Sir John Hawkley's temper. Tom had found an egg in some straw in a corner of the derelict smithy, but they had no means of cooking it. Then, when Sir John grudgingly agreed to eat it raw, the knight cracked it open to find that it was bad anyway. He threw the contents at Tom.

And still Alan had not appeared.

'I'd better go and look for him,' said Tom.

'I'm not waiting around here for these French dogs to give the inside of my neck an airing!' replied Sir John. He was busy turning his blue surcoat inside out and then folding it. 'That rogue Ralph can look after himself!'

Tom bit his lip, and managed to avoid giving the Knight of the Realm a lecture on the duties of master to servant – particularly a servant who has just saved his master's life. Instead, Tom told the Knight of the Realm that he was going to find Alan or, rather, Ralph and that they'd both catch up with Sir John before he reached the English army. Tom could hear himself sounding a lot more confident than he felt.

'You'll do no such thing!' exclaimed the Knight of the Realm, grabbing Tom round the neck and pushing him against the broken-down wall of the smithy. 'You'll carry that surcoat and follow me!'

The next thing Sir John did surprised Tom even more. He knelt down beside a muddy puddle (of which there were quite a few) and started rubbing the mud into his hair and skin.

'Odd way to wash,' Tom observed.

'Stop being clever and get some mud on you too,' snapped Sir John. 'Come on! Get that surcoat covered as well!' And Tom set to work smearing mud all over the inside of Sir John Hawkley's prized silk surcoat.

'Now!' exclaimed the knight, 'we need a couple of bits of wood and some string.'

By the time the sun's first pink rays had lit up the pink top of the main gate of the city of Peronne, Sir John Hawkley, Knight of the Realm of England, and his squire, Tom, were daubed from head to foot in mud and filth. They emerged from the derelict smithy banging a couple of bits of wood together as a clapper.

'You filthy lepers!' exclaimed the gatekeeper. 'Keep away from me!'

'God has punished us for our sins!' moaned Sir John. Tom was really most impressed with the great man's acting abilities. 'Please open up the gate and let us out!'

'I'm not opening up the gate just for a couple of dirty lepers like you!' returned the gatekeeper, who had clearly had less than a fair deal when God was portioning out human sympathy. 'You'll have to wait until some decent people want to pass through!'

'Damn him to blazes!' muttered Sir John under his breath. 'If he makes us wait we'll be caught like flies in the jam!'

Tom was unable to contribute much to this exchange because of his lack of French, however, he did what he could by going up close to the gatekeeper and grinning in his face.

'Get away! Get away!' cried the gatekeeper, and he grabbed his broom and started swinging it wildly so Tom had to dance out of the way.

'Hey! Stop that!' A voice rang out against the city walls, and the gatekeeper switched seamlessly into Grovelling Mode.

'Ah! Your Honour!' he tugged at his forelock. 'A fine day it is and one which we hope will bring your lordship great rewards and . . .'

'Hold your tongue and open up those gates for them!' Tom, who, in the course of dancing away, had fallen over backwards into the horse trough that always stood beside the city gate, looked up into the face of Sir Galahad de Ribemont. 'Let these poor wretches be! Their lot is bitter enough without your offensiveness!' Tom was mainly guessing what the knight was saying – but he was also beginning to recognize the odd word or two of French.

The gatekeeper started to open the gate with as bad a grace as he could get away with, and the knight turned to the small band of men-at-arms behind him.

'Search that old smithy!' he ordered. 'You three go down that street and the remainder come with me.'

'Hell's teeth! That was close!' muttered Sir John. 'They're searching for me already!' They were now waiting for the portcullis to be raised, when Tom gave a start.

'Sir John!' he hissed into the great knight's ear. 'Look!' But the noble knight was too preoccupied with the gate opening to notice that one of Sir Galahad's men had broken away from the group and was now riding up to them.

'Some alms for you!' said the young man. 'May God have mercy on you!' And with that Tom found himself holding up his hand to receive a coin from the one person in the whole city he was hoping to see. Alan winked as he dropped the coin into Tom's palm, and then turned his horse and rode on in the train of Sir Galahad de Ribemont.

Suddenly Tom was in a panic. The portcullis was fully up by now and Sir John Hawkley was doing a fine impression of a lame leper hobbling through the open gate into the wide world beyond. Tom sprang after him and tried to pull him back.

'Sir John! That was Alan! I mean Ralph!' he whispered. 'We can't leave him!'

'He seems to be doing pretty well for himself,' muttered Sir John. 'Got a new coat of livery, I notice.' It was true: Alan was sporting a jerkin in the blue and red of Sir Galahad's coat armour.

'But he doesn't want to be there! We can't desert him!' But Sir John was not stopping for anyone. Besides, the portcullis was starting to descend again. Tom hesitated for a moment. 'It'll probably stick again,' he heard a voice inside him saying. Then another voice told him that it wasn't worth standing directly underneath it to find out.

In fact, the portcullis did not stick on the way down this time. It crashed straight into the stone curb on the ground with a decisive clang. Tom, however, was well clear of it, hopping after Sir John Hawkley along the causeway across the moat, and away from the city of Peronne.

· 35 ·

Tom and Sir John Hawkley hobbled painfully down the road until they were out of sight of the city gate. There, by the milestone, Sir John suddenly abandoned his medically impressive theatrical performance, and threw himself down on the ground.

'Bag of the bull!' he groaned. 'My inside's as empty as a captain's coffer!' (It was a standing joke that when it came to paying men-at-arms, many a leader found himself unaccountably short of money.)

But Tom wasn't really listening to Sir John. He was trying to work out how in the world he was ever going to meet up with Alan again. 'It's odd,' Tom found himself thinking, 'despite all the scrapes he's got me into, despite all the stories he's spun me, despite the fact that he's a scoundrelly, trustless good-for-nothing – just like Sir John said that first time I met him – I'd really miss Alan. In fact more than that – I really like being with him.'

But how he was going to rescue his friend, he had no idea. Perhaps he could leave Alan a message by the milestone? But what would it say? Where could they meet? Where were they going?

While Tom was turning all this over in his mind, Sir

181

John had been deep in a monologue about the lack of food in his stomach. Tom was aware that the great man was getting more and more irritable by the minute, but it wasn't until he felt a hard blow across the back of his head that he realized quite how irritable Sir John had become.

'You lazy, dog-brained fly's dinner!' the knight was shouting. 'You haven't been listening to a word I've been saying! I said go and buy some victuals with that money you were given!' There was a baker's cart trundling along the road, heading for the town.

Tom leapt up and hailed the baker's man, and before Sir John could think of another curse, Tom had negotiated a large pie for the great man. He was just about to hand over the coin that Alan had given him, when he stopped and looked at it.

'For goodness' sake! Give him the money!' yelled Sir John. 'My stomach's yawning like the pit of hell! What are you looking at?'

'I can't wait around all day!' exclaimed the pie-man. 'Do you want the pie or not?'

'Of course he does!' exclaimed Sir John. 'Give him the money, Sam!'

'Wait a moment!' cried Tom. 'I just can't read the last word . . .'

But Sir John had snatched the coin out of Tom's hand. 'You don't *read* coins!' the great man was shouting. 'You buy pies with them!' And he flung it at the baker's man and took the pie.

'Oh please!' cried Tom. 'Give the coin back!'

'You must be joking!' exclaimed the baker's man. 'He's almost finished the pie already!' And it was true.

The moment the pie was in Sir John's hand, it was in his mouth, and the moment it was in his mouth, it was almost entirely consumed!

The baker's man put the coin away in his purse, and started to trundle the cart up the hill in the direction of the city. But Tom ran beside him.

'I just want to look at it! I'll give it you back!' he pleaded.

The baker's man gave him an old-fashioned look. 'What are you wanting now?' he demanded. Neither Tom nor the baker's man really understood each other's language, but each got the gist of what the other was saying. And now Tom was performing an elaborate pantomime. The baker's man was sufficiently amused to put his cart down for a moment and stop and look.

'You want me . . .' said the baker's man, 'to give you back the coin . . .'

Tom nodded 'yes', and went on with the mime.

'You want to look at it . . .'

Tom nodded again.

'And then you'll give it me back?' said the baker's man.

Tom nodded yet again.

'I wasn't born yesterday!' said the baker's man, and even though he didn't mime a single word of it, Tom knew what he was saying. The baker's man was just about to pick the cart up again, when Sir John cut in. He had finished the pie and was in a slightly more receptive mood.

'What is it, Sam? Why d'you want to look at the coin?'

'He's scratched on it!'

'The baker's man?'

'No! Alan! Ralph! He's scratched a message on the coin! But I didn't have time to make it all out!' All the time Tom had been trying to think of how to leave a message for Alan, it had never occurred to him that Alan had already given *him* a message.

Sir John didn't waste time with words; he grabbed the baker's man, slipped the fellow's knife out of his belt and held it to his throat. The baker's man, for his part, didn't waste time with words either, he dipped into his purse and handed the coin back to Tom.

'That's not the one!' cried Tom.

The next minute they had the baker's purse emptied out on the road and they were scrabbling through the pile of coins looking for the one that Alan had given Tom.

'Why in the devil's name didn't you tell me that good-for-nothing had passed you a message!' grumbled Sir John. Tom didn't reply; he'd just found the coin. And now he examined it closely he could read, hurriedly scratched on to the surface: '2 M 2 NIT'.

'He didn't have much time!' Tom felt surprisingly defensive on Alan's behalf. 'Anyway it was a brilliant idea to scratch a message on a coin!'

'It's not "brilliant" if you give someone a message they can't understand,' replied Sir John. 'It's something more like "stupid". Yes. I think that's the word I'd choose – "stone-dead, chicken-brained stupid"!' Sir John hated puzzles.

'Who said we can't understand it?' asked Tom. They had left the baker's man some way behind and were already half a mile down the road on their way to . . . well, Tom wasn't quite sure where they were on their way to, but he hoped Sir John knew.

'Well, if we can understand it,' Sir John continued, 'what does it say?'

'We've just got to work at it,' explained Tom. 'It's like a riddle.'

'We haven't got time to be messing about with riddles!' moaned Sir John, plonking himself down on the new milestone they'd just reached. 'We've got to get to the King's army before nightfall and we don't have horses, we don't have arms and we look like beggars! We are in one great load of horses' . . .'

But he never finished because Tom suddenly interrupted, even though he knew that you should never interrupt Sir John. 'You're sitting on it!' Tom exclaimed.

'The leg of pork?!' exclaimed Sir John. It has to be explained at this point that although Sir John Hawkley had been talking about their desperate situation he was actually thinking about where they could get some more food from – a leg of pork, for instance, roasted well, with crackling round the outside and juices dribbling down into his beard.

'No!' exclaimed Tom. 'The answer!'

Sir John looked down at the milestone he was sitting on. It read: 'Peronne 2 m'.

'What are you talking about?' he muttered.

'Alan's message: "2 M 2 NIT" – he's saying: he'll meet us at the "2nd milestone" – "2 NIT" – to-night! It was only a small coin – he didn't have room to put any more.'

Now whether Sir John had already worked this out or not, Tom wasn't quite sure, but the great man didn't say a word. He simply stretched himself out on the ground, put his feet up on the milestone and went to sleep.

'You might have said "Clever old Alan – er – Ralph" or even "clever old Tom, for working it out"!' thought Tom, but he didn't say anything. He squatted down beside the road and waited for whatever was going to happen next.

· 37 ·

Towards evening, Sir John Hawkley awoke in a very poor mood. The ground was wet. His skin was itching. He was covered in mud. And he was *hungry* again. The first person he turned on was Tom.

'Get your spotty backside off that grass and go and fetch me some victuals!' he growled. Now you might have expected Tom to be rather dismayed by this command, for after all, as he looked around that dismal, rain-soaked landscape, where the ground seemed to run away from him on all sides, and where people seemed like insects, the chance of finding any food would have seemed extremely remote. Tom, however, grinned at Sir John and said:

'Right you are, Sir John! How about this? One piece of cheese. One piece of bread. One garlic sausage. One flask of cider.'

You see, Tom had not been idle all day. Sitting by the roadside, looking for all the world like a poor leper boy, Tom had found himself an object of compassion to many of the travellers who made their way to or from the city of Peronne. He noticed that those who gave him anything were usually the ones who looked as if they most needed it themselves. It is true that the flask of cider had come from an attendant in the retinue of a nobleman who had passed by earlier in the morning, but generally Tom found it was the footsore and weary village-folk who had taken pity on his predicament. And Tom had seen no reason to argue with their better feelings. 'I may not really be a poor leper boy, as they think, but I certainly need everything they can give me,' he had reasoned.

And so Tom had crouched there all day, beside the milestone and the snoring carcass of Sir John, begging.

He had never realized being a beggar was such hard work. His back ached from being hunched up in a suitably pitiable posture all day, and his mind ached from the looks of disgust that he received from many passers-by. But there were one or two who were kind enough to speak to him. And that was another thing that Tom had spent his day doing – picking up words and phrases of French.

Sir John, however, gave all this not a single thought. He had already taken over the proceeds of Tom's day's work and was now earnestly engaged in the task of scoffing his way through them.

Night was falling by the time Sir John had eaten as much as he possibly could, and he was just beginning to complain that the cider was finished, when Tom heard hoof-beats approaching through the darkness.

'Alan!' he whispered to himself. 'And about time too!'

The hoof-beats drew closer and closer, until Tom could make out a figure in the dimness. Tom stepped out into the road. 'Alan!' he said again, 'we're over here!'

Alan didn't reply. He just kept riding towards Tom until he drew level with him. Then, before Tom could utter a word of greeting, he felt a sharp crack across the side of his head. He fell backwards and heard Sir John swear in the darkness. The next moment he was dimly aware of Alan's figure, leaning down from the horse with a raised sword.

Now a lot of questions raced through Tom's mind all at once, but he didn't feel like asking any of them just then – he simply rolled under the horses' legs as fast as he could, and the sword slashed into the ground which Tom had just vacated. Then as Alan (was it really Alan doing this?) tried to pull the blade out of the earth, Tom saw the dark mass of Sir John Hawkley leap on to the horse and the two figures toppled over on to the ground. The horse reared and Tom had to scramble out of the way again as it stamped its hooves and then galloped off, leaving Sir John and Alan (it couldn't really be Alan, could it?) grappling with each other for dear life.

A few moments of struggle and suddenly Alan gave a gasp. There was a deadly silence, before Sir John spoke: 'That'll teach you.' He stood up and wiped blood off his dagger. Tom looked at Alan and was relieved to find that – as he'd come to suspect – it wasn't Alan after all. It was a dark man with a moustache who gasped and tried to wheeze out a few words that Tom didn't recognize but which he knew meant 'Help me!'

Tom couldn't see very much, for the night was thick and impenetrable, but he had the impression of a damp blackness spreading over the man's front. And a strange feeling swept over Tom: even though this stranger had just tried to kill him, a terrible pity wrenched Tom by the shoulders and made him kneel beside the man and take his head in his hands. The man's hands clawed at the air like a creature drowning. Tom had no idea whether the man was trying desperately to get up or still trying to attack him, but he didn't care – he was overwhelmed by a compassion that shut out everything else.

'Leave him be!' growled Sir John Hawkley. But Tom couldn't – he tried to stop the blood, he tried to raise the man's head, but he knew it was useless, and all the time Tom was shaking his own head at the inexplicable pointlessness of what had just taken place.

'I always thought Life and Death were things that were announced by trumpets or the chorus entering stage left,' Tom found himself thinking, 'I never realized they might happen shabbily in the night for no apparent reason.'

At that moment more hoof-beats were heard, and Sir John stood up. It was Alan leading two spare horses.

'Quick!' Alan was excited and nervous. 'I think they may have heard me. Let's get out of here!'

'What about him?' Tom nodded at the man who had rolled over and was now panting into the earth. Alan peered at him. He gave a low whistle.

'It's one of Sir Galahad's men. They must have sent a search party out already! Come on!' And with that, Alan spurred his horse into the night and Sir John Hawkley and Tom scrambled on to their horses and followed after him.

· 38 ·

'I still don't understand why he attacked me,' said Tom. 'I was just sitting there looking like a poor leper.' Tom had just taken all his dirty clothes off and was about to follow Sir John Hawkley into the river.

'It's war-time,' said Alan. 'People do things that they wouldn't do at any other time. Some men kill just because they can and nobody can stop them.'

Sir John was singing at the top of his voice as he splashed around in the shallow water, rubbing mud out of his skin and hair. 'Sir John wouldn't do a thing like that – would he?' murmured Tom. Alan shrugged and gave Tom a shove so that he toppled off the bank into the flowing water.

'Ah! It's cold!' yelled Tom.'Aren't you coming in?'

'I'm not dirty,' said Alan.

'But it's fine!' laughed Tom, and he splashed Alan. 'Come on! Get your clothes off!'

But Alan shook his head. 'I'll just watch,' he said, but Tom had grabbed hold of his leg and was pulling him in anyhow. 'Stop it!' cried Alan. 'I'm not going in!'

'Oh yes you are!' cried Tom, and he pulled and tugged, but Alan fought back with surprising strength

191

and suddenly hit Tom hard in the face. Tom let go and Alan sprang back.

'Ow!' said Tom. 'What's the matter with you?'

Alan was glaring at him: 'I said I didn't want to go in,' he said. 'I don't want to get these clothes wet.'

'Then take them off,' said Tom.

'No!' shouted Alan. He really seemed quite angry, but Tom didn't have time to be more surprised, because he'd just felt himself grabbed around the neck and he was now threshing about under water. When he emerged, water filled his eyes and nose and mouth and Sir John Hawkley's raucous laugh filled his ears.

'Caught you napping there!' cried the great man. 'Always have to be on the alert!' he said. 'That's the name of this game!' The words were scarcely out of his mouth when they saw the horsemen on the other side of the river. There were about six of them – knights in armour galloping along the road in a cloud of steam and flying dirt.

'Satan's pimples!' muttered Sir John, as he heaved his weight up on to the bank. 'Have they seen us?'

'I don't think so,' replied Alan, who was pulling some new clothes out of a pack that was strapped to one of the horses.

Sir John was hurriedly drying himself on an old cloth that Alan had handed him. The next minute he was scrambling into a fine costume of gold, blue and red. Tom picked up the cloth that Sir John had dropped in the mud and tried to dry himself, but it was too wet. The next moment Alan threw him another set of clothes in the same colours as Sir John's.

'Where did these come from?' Tom whispered.

'Where d'you think?' said Alan. 'Hurry up!'

By the time Tom had dressed, his two companions had already driven their horses into the river and were half-way across.

Tom, who had imagined all the rush had been to *hide* from the horsemen on the other side, was a bit taken aback. His horse seemed equally uncertain about the manoeuvre and kept telling Tom that it much preferred the riverbank they had just left. It did this by turning around and heading back for the bank behind them. Tom replied each time, by forcing its head back towards the far bank, with the result that they kept turning in circles in the middle of the river, while Alan and Sir John reached the other side.

'Help!' cried Tom. But his companions were off, chasing after the horsemen who had already disappeared down the road. Tom's horse seemed to take this as a personal insult and it suddenly plunged through the river, scrambled on to the bank and charged off after its companions.

Some miles further down the road, they had still not caught up with the knights.

'By all the crippled saints!' exclaimed Sir John, 'They're going like bees after bears!'

'Who are they?' Tom ventured to ask.

'Some of them are wearing the colours of the Duke of Lancaster,' said Alan. 'They'll take us to the main English army.'

And off they set again.

They hadn't ridden for more than another couple of miles, when Tom, who was bringing up the rear – a couple of hundred yards behind Sir John and Alan – happened to glance behind. A motion on the distant horizon caught his eye. At first he thought it was a forest moving in the wind that had just sprung up. But as he peered along the vast curve of the Earth that seemed to be squashed up against the vast curve of the sky, he realized it was something altogether more alarming.

He kicked the sides of his horse as hard as he could, and the horse coughed but did nothing to increase its speed. 'Sir John!' Tom yelled, and the horse flicked its ears, but neither Sir John nor Alan turned round. Tom's words were snatched away by the wind like husks at winnowing, and his fear fell heavy at his feet.

'Come on, horse! Please!' Tom wished he'd had time to become a better horseman. 'It's all that priest's fault!' he muttered. 'If he hadn't kept me locked up in his library day after day with my head stuck in a book, I'd have learnt to ride properly and I'd be able catch the others up and tell them we've got about fifty horsemen on our tail! Come on, you stupid horse! I'll give you a carrot! I'll give you a whole cartload of hay!'

This was clearly the wrong thing to say to the horse, for it came to a complete halt, tossed its head first one way and then the other, as if considering Tom's proposal, and then started to chew the grass at its feet.

Tom turned around. He could make out the horsemen in the distance quite distinctly now. He even imagined he could hear the rumble of their hooves. Tom kicked his mount in desperation.

'I might as well be sitting on a sack of bricks!' grumbled Tom. 'Come on! This is an *emergency*! Run! Gallop! Go! PLEASE!'

But the horse had clearly no idea what the word 'emergency' meant. As far as the horse was concerned, it was a pleasant enough day – if a bit blowy; it had grass at its feet and a human on its back of whom it had no fear and for whom it had no respect, and so it might as well idle the day away doing whatever it felt like doing.

Tom, on the other hand, could see Sir John and Alan getting further and further away and the fifty pursuers, who he was sure were Sir Galahad's men, getting closer and closer. Tom was just about to jump off the horse and run for it, when Alan suddenly wheeled around. In an instant he saw Tom's predicament and he saw the horsemen behind them. In another instant, he had spurred his horse, galloped back to where Tom was, seized the reins from him and whacked the horse firmly on the haunch. The horse reared and then took off after Sir John like a cat on fire, with Alan riding alongside shouting and cursing.

If ever you find yourself being chased by fifty men on horseback, I recommend that you find somewhere other than the plains of Picardy to do it – especially if each and every single one of your pursuers stands to gain six pieces of silver for capturing you dead or alive. The trouble with Picardy for events of this sort is that you can see for miles and there is nowhere to hide. Once Sir Galahad's men had Tom and his companions in their sights, there was no shaking them off. They could see wherever they turned off the road, or if they doubled back, or if they stopped to hide. There was no escape as long as they fled across that remorseless, flat landscape.

However, just before the small town of Chauny, they found themselves hurtling downhill into a valley along the bottom of which the River Oise meandered as if it had all the time in the world, and wasn't being chased by anybody (which of course it wasn't). Across the river, the countryside changed. It became hilly and eventually was swallowed up by the Forest of Saint-Gobain.

'Come on!' yelled Sir John, in what was probably one of the most unnecessary commands he ever uttered in his life. There was not a chance in Heaven that either Tom or Alan would not have 'come on' in the circumstances. In fact they were 'coming on' so desperately that they were actually in front of Sir John when he uttered those superfluous words.

Now the good people of the town of Chauny had just built themselves a bridge across the River Oise. They were extremely proud of it, and all three of our heroes would have agreed that the bridge did make crossing the river much quicker and drier. There was one snag, however, and that was that the good people of Chauny were still paying for the construction of the bridge, and this involved collecting tolls from anyone who wished to go across it.

Tom was the first to spot the bridge-keeper. He was a large fellow with a large stomach, and he was busily engaged in eating his lunch out of a box which he had balanced on the parapet of the bridge. As soon as he saw the three friends racing down the High Street towards him, however, he dropped the piece of food he had in his hand and leapt into the middle of the bridge.

'Damn him to the hottest pit in Hell!' roared Sir John. And he spurred his horse on, riding straight for the fellow, and yelling 'Eat my hooves!' Alan followed suit, and Tom, who had fallen behind at this point, did his best to keep up. For some reason all three of them found themselves screaming: 'Eat our hooves! Eat our hooves!'

Now the bridge-keeper considered himself a bit of a

gourmet; but he wasn't fool enough to stand in the way of three desperate horsemen, no matter what gastronomic treat they were offering. The moment he realized that their *plat du jour* was still on their horses' legs, he leapt to one side, but as luck would have it he managed to grab Tom's bridle as they thundered past. The horse reared and Tom toppled off. The next minute the bridge-keeper was on him, with a strong arm around his neck.

Tom thought of yelling 'Help!' but decided to save his breath, especially since the bridge-keeper had his hand around Tom's throat and was squeezing out what little breath hadn't been knocked out of him by the fall. Tom twisted around, in a blind panic, and suddenly found the bridge-keeper's thumb sticking up under his nose. In a flash he had bitten it. The bridge-keeper yelped and let go for a split second, and Tom dived over the parapet of the newly-built bridge.

'Uh-oh!' thought Tom, 'I still can't swim!' It was too late, however, since he was already plunging downwards towards the river – in the way one tends to if one has just jumped off a bridge. As soon as Tom landed in the river, however, the last thing on his mind was his ability to swim. This was because he had just made the following discovery: rivers are like a lot of children – they love playing with mud. The River Oise certainly had had plenty of time, in its meanderings, to construct really interesting shapes and bumps and islands out of the mud that abounded along its course. And it had managed to build a particularly fine bank of mud exactly where Tom happened to land.

It was a soft, clinging sort of mud, and Tom went straight into it up to his waist. The bridge-keeper looked

over the parapet of the bridge and shouted something that Tom took to mean: 'Run along, my dear chap, and enjoy the rest of your life in peace and comfort!' although he knew the bridge-keeper was more likely to be shouting: 'I'll eat your tonsils on toast! I'll fry your liver for breakfast!'

Tom tried to pull himself out of the mud, but he seemed to sink in the more he struggled. And all the time he was thinking: 'Sir Galahad's men are getting closer! This is it! I'm finished!'

'I'll griddle your kidneys!' yelled the bridge-keeper. Tom looked up and was about to ask him to speak more slowly, when he noticed a piece of rope hanging from some scaffolding. With a supreme effort, Tom lunged, caught the rope, and started to haul himself up out of the mud.

By the time he had clambered on to the scaffolding that still clung to the underside of the bridge, he could hear the thunder of distant hooves, and he knew that Sir Galahad's search party was already nearing the town.

'Situation . . . Alternatives . . . Action!' thought Tom. 'Situation: "Help!". Alternatives: "Uh-oh!" or "Ohhh!". Action: "Aaaaaaarghhh!".' He kept on muttering this under his breath as he swung along the scaffolding, with his feet trailing in the waters of the river, making for the other side. He had no idea he was actually going to escape, and it was only as his feet landed on the far bank, that he suddenly saw the first glimmering of hope.

Alan had caught Tom's horse and was waiting there with it – shouting encouragement at Tom. This glimmering of hope, however, disappeared at the same moment that Alan yelled 'HURRY!' The look of fear in

Alan's eyes made Tom turn just in time to see, behind them, the militia of the town of Chauny arrive on the other side of the bridge. They were presenting pikes and halberds, and the bridge-keeper was gesticulating in the direction of Tom and Alan.

The militiamen started to swarm across the bridge.

'COME ON!' shouted Alan.

'I CAN'T!' Tom shouted back. He had already leapt on to his horse and was digging his heels into the horse's flanks as hard as he could, but the horse simply lowered its head and started to graze.

'How come I get the only horse in France that doesn't have any sense of urgency?' yelled Tom.

'Just dig your heels in!' yelled Alan

'I AM!' yelled Tom.

The militiamen had crossed the bridge, by this time, and were yelling and shouting blood-curdling threats as they ran towards the boys, brandishing their pikes and halberds. Without more ado, Alan grabbed Tom's bridle, yanked the horse's head up and away he went, dragging Tom's horse with him.

At that same moment, Sir Galahad's men appeared at the far end of the High Street. A shout went up from the bridge-keeper, and the militiamen turned, looked confused for a few moments and then ran back across the bridge. Faced with the choice between tolls from three English marauders and the tolls from fifty French knights on horseback, the militiamen knew their duty – it was the sort of money that could finish off paying for the bridge.

So, as Tom and Alan sped unhindered after the diminishing figure of Sir John, the bridge-keeper and his militia bravely lined up to block Sir Galahad's passage across the bridge. If Tom and Alan had been inclined to stop and watch what happened they would have seen tempers rise as Sir Galahad demanded free passage. They would have seen righteous indignation explode as the bridge-keeper demanded the full fee – plus a surcharge for every man-at-arms. They would have seen impatience get the better of one of Sir Galahad's knights as he spurred his horse into the river – only to make the same fascinating discovery that Tom had made, as man and beast sank into the soft mud, weighed down by armour and weapons. They would have seen the villagers gather round to laugh, as Sir Galahad's men concentrated their efforts on rescuing their comrade from the mud but instead found themselves one by one getting stuck in it too.

And, if Tom and his friends hadn't been a couple of miles away by this time, they would also have seen the bridge-keeper secretly celebrate his impending victory by sneaking over to his lunch-box and resuming his meal that had been so rudely interrupted. His lunch, on that particular day, happened to be one of the specialities of the region that he was particularly fond of. In French it was called *pieds-de-porc*. Tom would have called them 'pig's trotters'.

So you see, in the end, the keeper of the bridge at Chauny *did* eat hooves after all.

· 40 ·

'Bag my bones for Saint-Thomas!' exclaimed Sir John, and Tom was just about to ask the noble knight what this particular expression meant, when he breasted the hill on which Sir John and Alan were already standing and every thought vanished from his head. Tom found himself gazing down across a wide plain. In the distance a great city stood on a high plateau, with the soaring towers of a vast cathedral reaching up into the sky. But the part of the vista that took away Tom's breath and which had occasioned Sir John to make his remark, lay directly below them in the foreground. It was not a geological feature.

'That's the Duke of Lancaster's army or I'm meat for the crows at Christmas!' growled Sir John.

'At blooming last!' said Alan.

'Gosh!' said Tom.

Below them straggled a column of several thousand human beings: two thousand knights on horseback, followed by infantrymen, yeomen, archers, squires, pikemen, cooks, marshals, heralds, grooms, miners, engineers and blacksmiths. At their head marched the pioneers with spades and picks, ready to level the road

for the carriages. In the rear came a gaggle of women and children following the wagons.

Tom had never seen so many people in his whole life as were that day gathered on the plain at Laon in this army of the Duke of Lancaster.

That evening, Tom couldn't help feeling even more uncomfortable than he usually did when Sir John was in high spirits. He looked across at Alan in the flickering firelight. Even he appeared to be nervous and on edge. Sir John was regaling the people gathered around their fire with the full, unexpurgated and unabridged story of his last encounter with the French.

'And so I pulled my sword out and both cowardly rogues fell to the ground, while the treacherous dog who had crept up behind me coughed his last with my dagger in his ribs . . .' This was a fair sample of Sir John's narrative style at this moment, and when Tom caught

Alan's eye, they both eased themselves out of the circle
of light and huddled up together in the shadows.

'Great bell-ringing, by the way,' remarked Tom. 'It
certainly saved Sir John's bacon.'

'Thanks,' said Alan.

'What happened to you afterwards? I tried to get Sir
John to look for you – but he was in a bit of a state.'

Alan grinned. 'A bit hairy!' he said. 'I was just getting
out of the belfry, when these fellows grabbed me. Most
of them wanted to hang me then and there, alongside Sir
John, but one of them was from Sir Galahad's party. He
said they had to take me up to Sir Galahad. Luckily for
me! Sir Galahad recognized me, and told them they'd
made a mistake. Next thing I knew, he'd given me a set
of livery and a horse and told me I was to consider
myself in his service. Well I didn't argue. I just waited for
the right moment, and slipped away with whatever else
I could get my hands on. Doesn't fit you too badly.' He
smoothed Tom's suit as he spoke.

'You did fantastically!' Tom was full of admiration for his friend. Yet Alan was so modest about it all, it made Tom want to shake him. 'Not that his lordship showed any appreciation whatsoever.'

'Huh – Sir John's not a great one for thanks,' grinned Alan.

'You can say that again,' said Tom frowning. Then his face suddenly lit up. 'What'll happen tomorrow?' he asked.

'If the weather holds, the Duke will call the assault.'

'Are we going to try and take the city?' asked Tom.

'That's what everyone's saying,' said Alan.

'You don't look very happy about it,' said Tom.

'What's there to be happy about?'

'Well, isn't this what being a knight's all about?' exclaimed Tom. 'Riding into battle, banners flying, to vanquish your enemies, fighting for the right?' Tom suddenly looked six years old, his eyes were shining and he could have sworn he was talking to his sister Katie and that they were sitting around the fireside at home, with their mother humming to herself as she span, and their father winding cord around the handle of his old scythe.

Alan shrugged. 'You'll see,' he said. Then he put his arm around Tom, and pulled the blanket up over them both. Tom rested his head on Alan's shoulder. But as his eyes began to close, his mind kept going back to the strange feeling that he'd been talking to Katie. 'But of course,' he yawned to himself in his dreaming, 'if this were Katie, I would have my arm around *her* . . .' and that is probably where he fell fast asleep.

41

The next day was bright. The camp was all a-bustle and the horns were sounding. Tom awoke to find Alan already up and strapping Sir John into his armour – Sir John referred to it as 'his' armour, although Tom recognized it as belonging to one of Sir Galahad de Ribemont's men. Sir John's eyes were blood-shot and he was swearing a little more than usual, but Tom suddenly felt his heart race as he remembered this was the great day. The Duke of Lancaster himself was to lead an assault on the great city of Laon.

'By tonight we'll be the masters of that damned city,' grinned Sir John, 'and our fortunes will be made!' His laugh smelt of pickled herrings. 'There's rich pickings, I hear! Rich pickings!' The great man took another swig of beer, as Alan pulled the straps tight on his mail shirt.

Tom wanted to make himself useful. He also wanted to know what role he was to play in the day, but before he could ask Alan, he heard a cacophony of horns sounding.

'Damn my blisters!' exclaimed Sir John. 'They're starting! Hurry up there, Ralph! You're as slow as setting cheese!'

Tom gazed up at the great city of Laon. It stood there

on its high plateau, and the majestic towers of the cathedral and the high walls around the city seemed totally aloof from and oblivious to the preparations of the army down below. 'Perhaps they haven't noticed we're here!' thought Tom, and then dismissed the idea. But he couldn't help thinking that the great city looked distinctly unworried by the terrible threat to it that was fermenting on the plain below.

The high plateau on which the great city of Laon still stands is about six hundred feet high. It curves round in a huge crescent, with steep slopes – sometimes almost cliffs – on all sides. Here is an old map of the city as it was in 1359:

At the time when Tom found himself in the Duke of Lancaster's army, camped under its walls, the city had

A – Abbey of
Saint-Vincent.
B – La Villette
Saint Vincent.
C – Cathedral
and City of
LAON

LAON
en Picardie

only four ways in. Each was guarded by a heavily fortified gate and had only a narrow track leading up to it. If you had asked Tom how on earth an army – even one the size of the Duke of Lancaster's – could possibly climb those steep slopes, and scale those grim walls, he would have told you that he had no idea whatsoever.

Sir John Hawkley, on the other hand, seemed to have no doubts at all. 'Wine and wassail tonight!' he kept shouting. Alan had managed to get the knight on to his horse, and the great man whirled it around and rode off into the mounting pandemonium around them.

'Wait, Sir John!' yelled Alan. 'You haven't got your short sword . . .' but it was too late. Sir John had disappeared. Alan turned to Tom. 'I'll have to go after him,' he said.

'What about me?' asked Tom. 'What do I do?'

'You stay out of the way,' said Alan quite severely.

'But . . . I want to join in!' cried Tom. 'It's what I've always wanted to do!'

'Tom,' said Alan, suddenly very serious, 'this is not a game. This is a real-life battle. People will get killed. It's not fun. It's deadly serious.' Alan had both his hands on Tom's shoulders.

'But I've got to learn!' cried Tom. 'You've got to let me go with you.'

'My job is to find Sir John, give him his short sword and hold his horse when he goes into the attack,' said Alan. 'Your job is to stay here and guard the rest of the equipment; most people get rich in battle by pinching stuff from their own side.'

'But . . .' began Tom.

'That's your job,' said Alan, 'and besides . . .' he

added, looking Tom directly in the eyes, 'I don't want you getting hurt.' The next moment he was gone too, and Tom was left alone, sitting on the two packs that had been unslung from the other horses. He put his chin in his hands and did something odd – he began to cry.

The drums had now started, and shrill pipes were sounding, and it seemed as if the whole army were surging up the steep slopes around the city of Laon. And the tears poured down Tom's face. They were tears of frustration – to be so near to what he had dreamed about for so long and to be denied it. They were tears of anger that his friend had treated him as if he were a child. And they were also tears of sadness to see Alan go into all that danger – risking his own life for that of Sir John.

Tom stared at the confusion around him in amazement – he had not realized Alan meant so much to him, or that Sir John meant so little.

An hour or so later, Tom was puzzled. He had spotted the banner of the Duke some time before, and was surprised to see it being carried not towards the great bastion of the citadel, under the towers of the cathedral, but towards the middle of the plateau, which was slightly lower than the rest and where there weren't any fortifications.

'I suppose it makes sense,' thought Tom. 'Obviously you don't attack the most difficult point – you go for the soft spot. The middle of the plateau will be far easier to take, and then once he's up there, the Duke will launch his attack on the city itself.'

Tom found his mind searching through some of the old books he'd read with the priest back home. There was one he remembered, about the theory of battles and sieges, and as he sat there watching the assault on Laon from the distance, he began remembering the things that had been written in that book so long ago . . .

'That's the village of La Villette Saint-Vincent,' said a voice behind him in English. Tom turned and found a girl, slightly older than himself, standing beside him. She was pointing to the unprotected middle of the plateau, up towards which the army was now swarming.

'How do you know?' asked Tom.

'My father has told me everything about this place.'

'Who's your father?' asked Tom, but the girl didn't seem to have heard him. Her hand absent-mindedly stroked her blonde hair that was tied into a braid and hung down her back.

'That's the Cathedral,' she said.

'Funny I thought it was the duck-pond,' said Tom. 'It must be those towers that had me fooled.'

The girl laughed. One of her teeth was slightly chipped. 'And the other end is the Abbey of Saint-Vincent,' she said.

'Of course our duck-pond back home has much bigger towers than those. It's one of the finest duck-ponds in Britain.'

'I wish I could be up there fighting,' said the girl.

'So do I,' said Tom.

The girl came round and sat beside Tom on the other pack. 'Why aren't you?' she asked.

'Why aren't *you*?' replied Tom.

'Don't be daft, I'm a girl,' said the girl. 'They don't let women go into battle.'

Tom sighed. 'And I've got to look after the equipment. Otherwise I'd be there.'

They sat side by side for some time, gazing across at the rising tide of men-at-arms that was now almost lapping the top of the plateau, and would soon flood the village of La Villette.

'My father says this is all a waste of time,' said the girl.

'Who's your father to say that?' Tom was quite indignant. He could see the Duke's banner waving at the top of the slope, encouraging the men forward, and something like an ache in the pit of his stomach told him he wanted more than anything else in the world to be up there in all that action.

'My father says the Duke of Lancaster could never take Laon – not in a year – not in sixty years – and certainly not with just two thousand men-at-arms,' said the girl.

'You don't know what you're talking about,' replied Tom. 'You've seen all those men! Nothing could stop them! It'll be wine and wassail tonight!'

'My father says the Duke of Lancaster is only doing this to keep his men occupied – otherwise they'd be causing trouble. The German mercenaries have been grumbling again about not being paid.'

'If I hear another word about what your father says, I'll personally go and strangle him – whoever he is,' thought Tom, but he said: 'Well I wish I was up there with them.'

'Why don't you go?' asked the girl.

'I told you . . .' Tom began, but she interrupted.

'I'll stay here and look after your stuff.'

Tom sat and looked at the girl. She had black eyes that seemed to sparkle as she returned his gaze. Suddenly Tom heard the whoops and hollering as the English swept over the top of the plateau. The ache in his stomach pushed Tom on to his feet. 'You will?' he exclaimed.

'Only don't be too long,' said the girl.

'That's really great of you!' said Tom, and he did something he hadn't done since he and Katie had been saying goodbye outside Old Molly's ramshackle cottage: he gave the girl a smacking kiss on the cheek.

'You're a champion!' he said.

'I'll expect you to do something for me,' said the girl.

'When I come back!' yelled Tom, and he was off, running with all his might towards the siege of Laon.

42

Nothing may be what it seems. Everything is not necessarily what you expect.

It took Tom about half an hour to race up the side of the plateau. All the way, the sounds of battle grew louder and closer. He still felt surprised that there seemed to be no reaction whatsoever from the city of Laon itself. It just stood there, high on the eastern end of the plateau, ignoring everything that was going on below and to the west – like a card-player not showing his hand.

Tom arrived at the top, out of breath but elated. Now, at last, he would find out what it was like to take part in a battle. He was carrying one of Sir John's pikes, and he felt he could give as good as he'd get. Somewhere, between the excitement and the exaltation, there was a primal fear grabbing at his gut, but he ignored it. He breasted the top with eyes bright, and braced himself for the scene of carnage and death that was about to greet him.

But it didn't.

There were no corpses littering the battlefield, streaked with blood. There were no mangled limbs or severed heads – nothing that Tom had to brace himself for at all. Knights and foot soldiers were running around screaming and yelling but at each other as much as anything. Occasionally one would turn and hit one of the buildings with his sword, but it was just frustration.

The village of La Villette Saint-Vincent consisted of thirty or forty peasant huts – mean little dwellings with poorly thatched roofs and mud walls. A few dogs were wandering around, and one or two pots and pans had fallen by the wayside, but the villagers had clearly evacuated the place, to seek shelter in the safety of the city, well before the English had arrived. Everything of value had been taken away and there was nothing much for the Duke of Lancaster's great army to do except for setting huts on fire, pulling doors off hinges and fighting amongst themselves – which they were now doing with a will.

Before Tom could feel the full weight of anticlimax, however, a horn rang out. The men-at-arms seemed to pull themselves together and started to assemble into some sort of order.

Suddenly, in the midst of them, Tom spotted Sir John Hawkley and Alan. They had somehow managed to ride both horses up to the plateau and they were now lining up amongst the wagons and men-at-arms in front of one of the great lords' banners. Tom ran up and caught Alan's sleeve.

'What are you doing here?' exclaimed Alan. 'Who's looking after the baggage?'

'It's all right,' said Tom, 'this girl said she'd keep an eye on it.'

'Tom! You idiot! She'll steal it all!'

'No she won't,' replied Tom. 'She's a friend.'

'Who is she?' Alan was really quite cross.

'I . . . er . . . I don't know,' replied Tom, but before Alan could reply, more horns started to sound.

'Are we going to attack the city now?' asked Tom.

Alan gave him an odd look: 'You must be joking,' he said. 'It's fortified to high heaven!'

'Then what on earth *are* we attacking?' Tom had no doubt they were about to attack something, for the drums had now taken up the beat.

By way of reply, Alan nodded to the opposite end of the plateau, where there were more fortified walls, smaller than those of the city, but still formidable. Behind the walls rose spires and turrets.

'What's that?' asked Tom.

'The Abbey of Saint Vincent,' replied Alan, and the whole army began to move along the narrow path that led towards it. There were steep drops on both sides, and the horses neighed and backed up so that the wagon-drivers had their work cut out to keep moving. Everyone else had to keep their eyes open to avoid the frightened animals and the swaying vehicles.

'I can't believe you left all our equipment unguarded,' muttered Alan.

'I didn't!' replied Tom.

'This "girl" . . . you don't even know who she is . . .'

'She's nice,' said Tom.

'"NICE"!' Alan was full of scorn. '"Nice" girls don't come on trips like this – "nice" girls stay at home learning to spin or having children!'

Tom couldn't think why Alan was so bitter. 'She seemed nice to me.'

'She seemed nice to you!' scoffed Alan. 'And what do you know about girls?'

'I've got a sister . . . at least I used to have a sister . . .'
Suddenly Katie and the village seemed a lifetime away.

'Listen, I know about girls,' said Alan, 'and I know this sweetheart who you think is so "nice" was just chatting you up to get her hands on our baggage.'

'You can't know that,' exclaimed Tom. 'You didn't meet her.'

'You shouldn't have left the bags! You disobeyed my orders!' shouted Alan.

Sir John Hawkley turned. 'Quiet in the back there! Keep some order, damn you, Ralph!'

They moved on for some time in silence. In front of them, across the narrowest neck of the plateau, loomed the main gate and walls that led to the abbey. As they got nearer, Tom suddenly heard a sound he half recognized although he'd never heard it before. The next moment he saw a cloud of arrows rise into the air from the other side of the gate. Tom stared in fascination. The arrows seemed to move across the sky so slowly . . . flying in perfect formation under the clouds, closer and closer . . . and Tom simply stood there, as if mesmerized – waiting to see where they would land – fascinated by the clean arc they described above him, getting closer and closer . . .

Suddenly Tom felt himself pulled hard to the ground, and he realized Alan had pushed him under the wagon they were walking beside, and not a moment too soon, for the arrows immediately thudded into the ground around them and the wagon above their heads. The wagon driver screamed and fell, clutching his shoulder.

There was another swishing sound, and another volley of arrows came over.

'There can't be many of them!' shouted Sir John from

under the safety of his shield. 'There'll be rich pickings inside! Mark my words!'

Tom's heart was beating fast. Suddenly he heard horns sounding, drums beating, and a manic yell went up from the Englishmen. The next moment, everyone was running at the abbey walls screaming and cursing.

Tom rolled out from under the wagon and to his surprise found that he too was running and screaming and cursing with the rest of them. Perhaps he felt that if he screamed and cursed hard enough, he'd kill the bitter taste that Alan's scolding about the bags had left in his mouth.

Once at the abbey, the engineers produced scaling ladders and began swarming up the walls. The next volley of arrows was less than half the size of the previous ones. 'They're on the run!' exclaimed Sir John, and suddenly he was elbowing his way to the front, desperate to be among the first to get into the abbey.

In fact the whole English army had, by this time, formed a sort of nightmare queue, with everyone fighting each other in their scramble to get into the abbey.

The volleys of arrows had now completely stopped, and Sir John had reached the top of the wall. 'Rich pickings!' he cried as he disappeared from view down on to the other side. The next moment, Tom felt a sharp blow on the back of his head, and found himself pushed aside. The gates of the abbey had begun to open, signalling a stampede among the English soldiers. The panic to get in and get at the riches inside was almost visible, but it took Tom totally by surprise, as he tried to pick himself up from the trampled ground.

Once on his feet, Tom found himself carried forward by the surging mass, until they burst through the narrow gate like a thousand corks from a single bottle.

Inside Tom realized they were not yet actually in the abbey, but in the small town that serviced it. The abbey itself lay beyond another set of walls. The English soldiers, however, were not concerned with such fine details, and they were already busy at their god-given task of stripping out anything of value from each and every building. The majority of them had made for the two great churches that stood outside the abbey grounds, while the rest were hard at work ripping furniture and fittings out of the houses. A few, however, had begun to attack the great doors of the abbey.

All the defence forces seemed to have made themselves scarce, although Tom could see one or two dead bodies, which he assumed (wrongly, as it happened) were defenders who had not been quick enough to escape.

Sir John had joined those who were trying to get into the abbey grounds, and he was among the first to break through as the great gates swung open. Tom and Alan followed in time to glimpse the frightened faces of two monks as they ran across the open ground in front of the abbey until a hail of arrows brought them to a stop. By the time Tom could cross the yard, the two monks were lying quite still, like two enormous hedgehogs, face down in the trodden earth.

The majority of the English soldiers were making for the great Abbey Church itself, but Sir John, whose experience in these matters Tom was sure he could trust, had side-stepped the main horde, and was at that moment trying to get into the refectory. Alan had joined him in

moments, and as Tom reached them the doors flew open and the three of them stumbled into the great dining hall of the Benedictine monks of the Abbey of Saint-Vincent.

Tom gawped. It was the largest room he had ever been in. The windows were large and studded with coloured glass. The ceiling was vaulted, and supported by slender columns. Around the walls were inscriptions and paintings, and down the centre ran three long wooden tables, whose polished oak shone in the gentle light. Tom could not believe that a ceiling could be that high, or that one wall could be that far away from another.

Sir John and Alan, however, didn't seem at all impressed with the architectural proportions of the place. They were too busy searching around behind tables and under cupboards, and it was only a matter of moments before Alan shouted: 'Found it!'

Sir John was at his side in a flash. In another flash they had the lid off the chest that Alan had discovered, and Sir John was almost singing with delight.

'Lookee! Lookeee!' he cried, and he began stuffing silver goblets and knives and spoons into his jerkin. Alan had produced a cloth and the two of them started throwing as much as they could into it, before a noise at the door made Sir John jump out of his skin.

'Who's there?' The voice of one of the Duke's sergeants rang across the refectory.

'Dogs of the Devil!' muttered Sir John. 'Quick, Ralph!' and the two of them hurriedly banged the lid back on the chest, and disappeared into the shadows at the far end of the refectory.

The sergeant was already running across the hall and it was only when he actually grabbed hold of Tom's neck that Tom decided the best thing he could do was to run too, but by then it was too late.

'Caught you, you little thief!' exclaimed the sergeant. 'What have you got in there?' And he started ripping open Tom's jerkin and, at the same time, pulled him into the light. 'Why!' he said, 'You're only a child!'

He dragged Tom towards the chest and kicked the lid off. It was now only half-full of silver. The sergeant turned to Tom. 'You know that all booty belongs to the King, don't you?' Tom shook his head. 'It all belongs to him,' repeated the sergeant. 'So if you find anything valuable, you must hand it in to me or to one of the other sergeants, d'you understand?' Tom nodded. 'Then we'll record what you've found and the Duke will give you your share, after the King's given him his.'

So that was how it worked, thought Tom. No wonder Sir John was in such a hurry.

'Now if you see that man who took the things from here,' – the sergeant had adopted a kindly-uncle manner – 'you must report him to me. D'you understand?'

Tom nodded in as gormless a way as he could manage, without laughing, and the sergeant released his arm. 'Now you run along,' said the sergeant. 'If you see another sergeant (he'll have a red ribbon on his arm), tell him I need help to carry this thing to safety before any more of those jackals land on it.'

So Tom hurried off in the direction in which Sir John and Alan had disappeared.

Tom found himself in a dark passageway. He could

hear voices at the far end, and he could see a ray of light seeping from underneath another closed door. This door proved to be locked, but he could hear Alan and Sir John whispering on the other side of it, so he knocked. The voices at once fell silent.

'It's me! Tom! Sam, I mean!' whispered Tom.

Cautiously the door opened, and Alan let Tom in, and re-locked the door. For the second time that day, Tom caught his breath as he walked into a room. But this time it wasn't the size of the room that filled him with awe, it was *what was in it*.

'I've never seen so many . . . I didn't even imagine there could be so many . . .' Tom sank to the floor with his mouth open.

'Don't just sit there! There's work to be done!' Sir John was in a state of heightened excitement. His jerkin still bulged with the stolen silverware, and he had a firm grip on the clothful of goblets.

'There's no way out of that door,' shouted Alan. He was exploring all the possible escape routes. 'We could make for the cloister, but the sergeants are everywhere. Tom! Go and look from the gallery up there!'

But Tom didn't hear him. Tom had been carried away by the contents of the room. His mind had suddenly been transported to other times and other places, and he had discovered that he had secretly been missing something that he didn't even think he liked in the first place.

For the room he now found himself in was a library. Not a library such as the village priest had back home; the priest's library consisted of one perhaps two books at most. This library was different.

If Tom could have counted them all, he would have been able to count eleven thousand volumes sitting on shelf after shelf – all round the room, and from the floor to the ceiling. There was even a gallery running around above their heads, with ladders up to it and more books stretching on up above that. And each book was secured to its shelf by a chain. Below the shelves was a sloping table that allowed you to read the book where it was. For in those far-off days, books were not printed, they were all written out by hand. Each one was unique and so valuable that it was never allowed outside the library.

Tom pulled a volume off the one of the shelves. It had been written in Latin some six hundred years ago and copied out some two hundred years later. As if mesmerized, Tom sat down and started to read. The here and now fell away from him. He could no longer hear the shouting and screaming from outside. He was deaf to the orders of the sergeants and the yells of the men, and the crashing of arms and armour and the running of feet. He was oblivious to Sir John Hawkley and Alan who had been yelling at him too, and he was equally unaware that one of the sergeants was now hammering on the door of the library, demanding that Sir John open it up.

Tom was reading: '*Omnem terrae ambitum . . . ad caeli spatium puncti constat* – The whole circle of our earth is but a dot compared to the vastness of the heavens.'

'Our only chance is to get through the cloisters and away round the back,' reported Alan 'but they're bound to spot us!'

'What we need is a diversion!' growled Sir John.

'Leave it to me,' said Alan. 'Diversions are my speciality.'

'No!' grinned Sir John. 'The usual way will do!' and he disappeared through a side door in the library.

Tom saw nothing of all this. He read on: '*Si aeternitatis infinita spatia pertractes, quid habes quod de nominis tui diuturnitate laeteris?* – If you really think about the infinite space of eternity, what pleasure can you take in the long life of your own name?'

'Tom! What are you doing?' Alan's voice broke Tom out of his reverie.

'I'd forgotten what it was like,' murmured Tom.

'What what was like?'

'To read,' replied Tom, his eyes starting to wander round the shelves of books.

The sergeant was now trying to barge the door open with his shoulder.

Alan looked at Tom with curiosity. 'What's it like?' he asked.

Tom sighed. 'It's like . . . not being blind . . . It's like . . . standing on the edge of a cliff and knowing you can fly.'

'Reading?' said Alan.

'Reading,' replied Tom. 'Look around you, Alan, all those books! I always thought being able to read would mean there were six or seven books I could read – a dozen at the most. I never dreamt there could be so many books! And each one of them is someone speaking to us from long ago. Each of those pages has a voice with something to tell us . . . without them we would be deaf to the past. Imagine! This whole room is

226

shouting at us! For those who can hear, this room contains everything they ever need to know . . .'

Alan looked around the room, and suddenly understood what it was like to be deaf. The sergeant had given up trying to barge the door in and had gone off to recruit help or to give his colleague a hand with the treasure chest.

'I wish *I* could read,' said Alan.

'And *I've* only just realized I'm glad I *can*!' exclaimed Tom. 'Walking in here . . . I suddenly saw that the whole world – more – is in books. It's like being able to see beyond the horizon! Look! I'll read you something!' And he pulled another volume off the shelf. He opened it at random and frowned.

'I can't read this to you,' said Tom.

'Why not?' Alan's interest was clearly quickened. 'Is it black magic or something?'

'It's in Greek,' said Tom. 'I don't even know the alphabet.'

At that moment, Sir John Hawkley burst through the door with a flaming torch. 'The best diversion in the world!' he exclaimed, and hurled the blazing brand across the library so it exploded against the far wall of books.

Tom stared for a few moments, although it felt as long as the six hundred years since Anicus Manlius Severinus Boethius put his pen to the book that Tom had been reading previously. Tom simply could not take in what Sir John had just done. Had the great man really just thrown a live, flaming torch into the heart of that wonderful, extraordinary place? As the six hundred years came to an end, Tom finally took in the fact that that was exactly what Sir John Hawkley, his lord and master, had done.

'No!' screamed Tom. And he hurled himself towards the flames which, by this time, were already licking up the dry shelves. Tom ripped off his jerkin and started beating at the fresh flames with it.

'What's that young idiot up to?' exclaimed Sir John.

'He's not an idiot, Sir John,' said Alan calmly.

'But what's he doing?' grumbled Sir John.

'He's trying to save the past,' said Alan, and he ran to Tom's side.

But there was nothing either of them could do. The library had been kept perfectly dry for a hundred years, so that the books would not perish. But now the very thing that had preserved them in the past turned them into easy kindling for Sir John's eager torch, and the flames took hold everywhere, as fast as Tom or Alan could beat at them with their jackets. Eventually Tom turned on Sir John.

'How could you?' Tears were streaming from his eyes and he didn't care.

'Satan's socks!' Sir John screamed back. 'It's a *diversion*! You ignorant know-nothing!'

'You're murdering them!'

'WHO?'

'They're irreplaceable! Some of them may be the only copies in existence! You're destroying knowledge! Life! Quick! We must save them!'

And before Alan could stop him, Tom was leaping around trying to pull the books off the shelves. Sir John, for his part, was going apoplectic. 'Has the boy gone mad?' he yelled at Alan. 'We've got to get out of here!'

But Alan too had joined Tom, trying to pull volume after volume off the shelves. But the very chains that had stopped them from being stolen in the past now stopped them from being rescued.

And still the flames rose higher, until they were licking the lofty roof of the library. And the fire reached out . . . covetously fingering the books on either side . . . selecting one . . . two . . . and then all of them for its own voracious reading . . . a reading that would mean no one else in the entire history of the world would ever get the chance to read that particular book again.

A window crackled and then burst in a shower of glass as the heat suddenly expanded the air in the room, and a blast of new fire erupted across the space, consuming stools and writing desks. Tom and Alan were hurled against the wall as they leapt back. Sir John screamed: 'Get out!' and he grabbed the clothful of silver goblets and headed for the door . . . But the flames flew across the ceiling as if to intercept him and thank him for giving them this unexpected outing.

Alan grabbed Tom's hand and yanked him towards the door. Loose pages were floating down from the ceiling where the raging fire had carried them, and Tom started grabbing at them, and stuffing them into his shirt. Alan didn't care whether Tom wanted to save even such an infinitesimal part of all that knowledge and wisdom from the past; he knew they had to get out of that developing inferno before they too became a part of the past – and a very small and charred part at that.

· 43 ·

Sir John's diversion was a resounding success. The conflagration he had started focused everyone's attention so completely, that Sir John and his team were able to slip through the cloisters and out of the abbey grounds, clutching their handful of silver goblets and cutlery without a single sergeant spotting them.

The moment they reached the horses, they scrambled off down the steep slope as fast as their steeds could slither and slide and stumble. And so they returned to the plain beneath the plateau of Laon.

In fact the whole siege of Laon was generally judged to be a resounding success. That night the Duke of Lancaster's camp rang to the stories of heroism, danger and daring that had taken place during that remarkable day. The pickings had, indeed, been rich – just as Sir John Hawkley had prophesied. The Duke's sergeants had recorded the treasures of the Abbey as they were loaded on to wagons and carried down the steep road from the plateau.

As a matter of fact that had been the only really dangerous bit of the whole enterprise, for the road, which the knights had avoided but which the wagons were forced to take, wound under the city of Laon and exposed the wagon-drivers to the arrows from the townspeople above. Only half a dozen wagoners had been killed, however, and most of the treasure safely reached the coffers of the Duke of Lancaster. It was, the Duke and his advisers felt, a thoroughly cost-effective exercise, and they had proclaimed throughout the camp a ration of free wine and beer for everyone – man, woman and child.

And so the night rang with toasts to the unparalleled generosity of Henry, Duke of Lancaster and his glorious leadership in battle.

Tom was a little surprised by all this. As far as he could see there hadn't actually been any battle. The English army had certainly killed a few defenceless stragglers up on the plateau, but for the most part the enemy had all locked themselves up in the city of Laon and steadfastly refused to fight anybody.

As for the 'Siege of Laon', which was the magic phrase on everybody's lips that night, they hadn't actually attacked Laon itself, but only the peasant village and the virtually undefended Abbey at the other end of the plateau.

Tom, however, didn't spend much time puzzling over these things; he was preoccupied with another problem altogether. He and Alan and Sir John had returned to their baggage to find that, as Alan had predicted, it wasn't there, and neither was the girl whom Tom had left in charge.

The effect of this discovery upon Sir John would have been a lot worse if he hadn't been in such a good mood, but, even so, the effect was bad enough. If there had been a roof, Sir John would have hit it. If there had been a handle there, Sir John would certainly have flown off it. There was, however, plenty of red in the camp, and Sir John saw it.

'You worthless piece of beetle poop!' he yelled as he grabbed Tom's hair. 'You toe-wart! You empty-headed, half-witted, under-brained, incompetent, cretinous, imbecile!' Quite frankly, Tom thought Sir John's gift for invective was not what it used to be. He excused the great man, however, on the grounds that he was so beside himself with rage that he couldn't think straight.

And Tom could nowadays tell quite accurately just *how* enraged Sir John was by the distance he travelled when Sir John hit him. A couple of feet indicated 'not amused'; four feet meant 'really shirty'; six feet showed 'sheer white-face fury'; and eight feet indicated that it wouldn't be at all safe to stay on the same planet as Sir John, at least until he cooled off.

In this instance, Tom reckoned he covered about seven and a half feet, and landed with his head inside an empty beer barrel. He managed to scramble to his feet even before Sir John could take another swig of beer, and made off on a search for the missing equipment. He hoped that, by the time he returned with it, Sir John would be too drunk to be able to hit him again. This latter hope was to be fulfilled. The search for the missing equipment, however, was to prove fruitless.

Tom combed the camp for the girl, but he didn't see so much as the braid of her hair. But the curious thing, Tom discovered, was that mixed up with his shame and anger at the girl, was some other feeling . . . He wasn't quite sure he liked the feeling, but it certainly made him want to see her again . . . He couldn't get out of his head the image of her black eyes and her quick smile whenever she looked at him. But the girl herself had vanished along with her smile, her eyes, and their luggage.

When Tom returned empty-handed, he was relieved to find that Sir John (fuelled no doubt by the Duke's free beer and wine) was back on form with his powers of invective. 'Satan's scab-licker!', 'Devil's dog-sore!' and 'Unfit for Hell!' were among the epithets that rolled effortlessly off the great man's lips that evening. But he was clearly in a good mood, for all that, because he didn't throw anything more than a few medium-sized rocks at Tom. For most of the time, he simply sat on his clothful of silverware and handed his mug to Alan for yet another free beer.

That night, however, when they had settled down to sleep as best they could, under a ragged bit of canvas awning, it was Alan who suddenly turned on Tom. 'Never, *never* trust a woman!' he hissed. 'I can't *believe* you fell for such an old trick! Was she so beautiful? Did she tell you how good-looking you were? I expect she fluttered her eyelashes at you and you went all weak at the knees? Did you?'

'No. It wasn't like that!' Tom was really taken off guard by his friend's intensity.

'So what *did* you talk about?' persisted Alan.

'As a matter of fact we talked about her father,' replied Tom, feeling more defensive than he thought he ought to feel. 'He said this whole siege is a waste of time – just a diversion to keep the men quiet.'

'And who's her father?' The scorn in Alan's voice made Tom want to curl up and go to sleep there and then.

'She didn't say.' Tom pulled the bit of blanket he'd

found closer round him and shivered. It had begun to rain. 'She said she wished she could join the battle.'

'Don't be stupid!' Alan was almost spitting. 'Girls don't want to be in battles.'

'This one did.' Tom's voice had gone quite wistful.

There was a dead pause. The sound of the fire crackling, the ripping snores of Sir John and the shouts of other drunken men around the camp mingled with the patter of the rain on the armour and canvas. Then Alan asked in a quieter voice: '*Was* she beautiful?'

'I don't know,' replied Tom. And with that he turned away and did a pretty good imitation of someone who had suddenly and unexpectedly fallen asleep.

But sleep eluded him for much of that night. Partly it was the cold and the rain, but mostly it was the great turmoil going on in his head.

In the first place he couldn't understand Alan. Of course he had a right to be angry, but there seemed to be such a scorn in his voice – as if he had suddenly written Tom off as a friend. And why was he so contemptuous of women? What secret ordeal had he suffered at the hands of a girl? For Tom could see no other reason why he should hate them as much as he appeared to. Alan had suddenly seemed to become a stranger – someone whose mind Tom could as little see into as he could into the darkened tents of the Duke's snoring camp.

The second thing that made Tom toss and turn in his pretend-sleep was the face of the girl – the girl who had conned him so effortlessly into handing over their equipment. He should hate the sight of her, hate the false smile, hate the deception in those black eyes that had encouraged him to do such a foolish thing . . . But that wasn't how Tom felt . . . It wasn't how he felt about her at all . . .

But as bad as each of these troubles was for Tom's peace of mind that night, there was yet a third thing that overshadowed everything else – even the wet and the cold.

The cause of this disquiet was certainly not wet nor was it in the least bit cold – quite the reverse – and if he raised his eyes he could still see it: high up there on the plateau of Laon, the magnificent library of the Abbey of Saint-Vincent, the home of eleven thousand books, the repository of centuries of thought, still blazed, lighting up the night sky like a beacon of lost dreams.

Tom stared at the distant flames, his mind still numbed by disbelief. To have had that storehouse of knowledge revealed to him so suddenly and then – equally suddenly – to have had it snatched away was almost more than Tom could face up to. Yet he lay there, in the rowdy night of the camp, trying to make sense of it all. But there was no sense to be made of it.

All that remained of all those thousands of books were the four pitiful pages that Tom had managed to stuff into his shirt. He now spread them out in front of him. Two of them contained writing – but in Greek. The other two pages, as luck would have it, were blank.

Sir John belched in his sleep. Tom's eyes flicked towards him. The great man didn't look very powerful, lying there oblivious to the world in his drunken stupor, and yet he had that day – single-handedly – obliterated eleven thousand voices calling from the past. He had wiped out a whole civilization's worth of knowledge in return for a cloth-full of silverware.

Tom suddenly discovered a feeling in himself that he had never known before . . . It was a bitter feeling . . . an angry feeling . . . Perhaps it was hatred . . . perhaps it was contempt . . .

'Everything's changing,' thought Tom. He suddenly sat up and looked around the camp, listening to the barking of the drunken soldiers, the quarrelling of the dogs. A fight had broken out some distance away and he could see two figures scuffling in front of one of the fires.

But in his mind's eye, Tom was staring at the frightened faces of the two monks as they ran in front of the Abbey that morning. Then he saw them again, dead as hedgehogs, lying in blood. It had shocked him – made him feel sick – but he knew he'd been prepared for the sight of death. He had always known, without thinking, that death was a part of war. The thing he had *not* been prepared for was the destruction of ideas.

He gazed at the plume of flames up on the plateau of Laon, and for the first time in his life, as far as he could remember, Tom was no longer certain what he wanted to be.

44

The day had broken over a new world as far as Tom was concerned. He felt as if someone had sneaked up to him in the night and replaced his old eyes with someone else's. He didn't know quite what effect this would have, but he looked round more warily than he would have done the day before.

The first thing his new eyes came to rest on was a figure he dimly recognized. He couldn't see the face, because a hood was pulled down low over it, but something in the way the man was kicking sleeping bodies awake, turning them over and then peering down at their faces, seemed awfully . . . awfully familiar. And then Tom heard it – the voice. The familiar unfamiliar accent.

Tom was on his feet in a flash, waking Sir John.

'Hang the dogs!' exclaimed Sir John, hitting out at Tom with his fists. But Tom grabbed both Sir John's arms and pinned them to the floor. The look of surprise in Sir John's face was all the breakfast Tom would get that day.

'Shut up!' Tom hissed in the great man's ear, 'And listen to me! The Priest's here! He's got three men and they're going round looking for someone. And I wouldn't be at all surprised if that someone was us.'

Sir John's face switched from utter surprise to utter surprise and back again.

'One at a time.' Tom suddenly found himself organizing everything. 'You go first with the silver, and don't run. Alan and I will follow as best we can.

'But it *can't* be him!' Sir John had finally found his voice. 'We left him for dead!'

'You *always* seem to be leaving him for dead! But I can tell you it's him. Quick! Now! While they've got their backs to us!'

He pulled Sir John to his unsteady feet, thrust the cloth of silver into his arms and pushed him away. The great man staggered through the lines of sleeping bodies. Tom fell back to the ground and turned to watch the Priest and his henchmen.

The four of them were working their way methodically through the lines. 'I bet *they'd* have found the girl who stole our things,' Tom muttered to himself as he kicked Alan.

'What?' Alan was awake instantly, and Tom outlined the situation.

'Don't look! He's staring at us . . . No! I think he's watching Sir John . . . But he hasn't recognized him . . . No . . . He's gone back to searching . . .'

'Situation – alternatives – action,' mumbled Alan.

'I've already done that,' said Tom. 'They're getting closer. We've got to get away without them spotting us.'

'Or make a run for it,' said Alan.

'Oh my goodness!' groaned Tom. The Priest and his men had changed direction. 'They're coming straight towards us!'

'Looks like we run for it!'

'But we'll have to leave all the stuff!'

'OK. Let's play dumb! Just lie low and hope they'll leave us alone.' Alan shut his eyes.

The Priest and his party were no more than a dozen sleeping bodies away. They were still examining the sleepers as they made their way, but they were definitely heading straight for the spot where Tom and Alan were lying.

It was at this moment that Tom suddenly developed a new enthusiasm for military discipline. It wasn't a subject he'd thought much about before, but a few seconds changed all that. As the Priest got nearer, and it became clear that nothing was going to stop them being discovered, the sharp notes of the Duke of Lancaster's trumpets suddenly rang out across the camp. Immediately, as if they'd been lying there just waiting for the *reveille* to sound, the men were up and on their feet. The whole camp turned from horizontal to vertical in a matter of a few seconds – or so it seemed to Tom. The net result, in any case, was that the Priest and his henchmen were suddenly lost in the instant forest of people.

Tom and Alan grabbed as much stuff as they could carry and bolted.

The great *rendezvous* took place a few miles down the road. Edward III's expedition had marched from Calais in three separate armies. One was led by his son, the Black Prince, another by the Duke of Lancaster and the third by the King himself. They were finally to meet together here in the Forest of Vauclair.

The Duke of Lancaster's army had stopped to rest on a hill. Below them Tom and Alan could see a great swathe cut through the forest as the King's army advanced towards the Abbey of Vauclair, which was to be the royal headquarters.

Tom had never seen anything like it. The pioneers had already made their way, hacking and clearing the forest, levelling the road for the rest to follow. Now there came five hundred knights in the van, banners flying, armour shining. Behind them came a thousand archers, followed by the King himself and his companions, surrounded by some three thousand men-at-arms and five thousand archers. Behind *them* the baggage train trailed some six miles into the distance – thousands upon thousands of carriages, wagons and carts.

Knowing the already ravaged state of France, where food was scarce and famine rattled its bones in every untilled field, King Edward of England had thought fit to bring enough provisions for his entire army. What's more he had brought hand-mills for grinding their corn and even mobile ovens to cook the food. It was the largest and best equipped army ever to cross the English Channel.

The sight should have made Tom's heart burst with pride – and it would have done twenty-four hours before. But today, he had his new eyes. His new eyes saw the frightened faces of two defenceless monks, running before every knight's charger. His new eyes saw a burning library in the flash of every spear. It was not the inspiring vision of Chivalry taking to the field that his new eyes saw, but Destruction on the move.

'Still no sign of him,' Alan appeared at Tom's shoulder. 'He's probably half-way to Paris by now.'

'What d'you mean?' Tom was genuinely shocked. 'Why would Sir John go to Paris?'

'Or London,' added Alan.

'But the armies have only just met up! The campaign's just beginning!'

Alan laughed. 'Sir John's got what he came for. Why should he stick around? He'll be wanting to find a dealer who'll give him a good price for all that silver he's run off with.'

'But he wouldn't just leave us to fend for ourselves!' exclaimed Tom.

Alan shrugged. 'Well he's done a pretty good impression of exactly that,' he said. 'Any sign of the Priest?' They had moved up the column so that they were now about a mile away from their old position, where the Priest had nearly caught them. But they were still uncertain as to whether he had actually spotted them or not.

Tom shook his head, and returned his gaze to the sight below. 'So what are we going to do? You always said that without a knight we were just a couple of beggar boys.'

'We're not quite that bad,' replied Alan. 'We're wearing a decent livery . . .'

'Belonging to a Frenchman,' Tom reminded him.

'Belonging to whoever we say it belongs to,' replied Alan. 'And besides, we've got a couple of horses and these,' and Alan pulled a small parcel out from his jerkin. It contained three silver knives and two spoons. 'I wasn't going to let Sir John get away with everything,' he smiled. 'But you're right. We still need to be in somebody's retinue. The question is, whose?'

A smile spread across Tom's face. 'I know,' he said.

Alan looked across at him. 'Uh-oh!' he said. 'I get a funny feeling when you smile like that, Tom.'

'If we're offering our services, let's go for the top!' grinned Tom. Alan followed Tom's gaze down across the King's army below, where camp sites were being marked out and argued over, to the knot of horsemen surrounded by crimson and gold banners and accompanied by drums and flutes, who were now making their way through the throng towards the Abbey of Vauclair.

'I hope you're not thinking what I think you're thinking,' murmured Alan.

But Tom was.

45

When the two boys arrived at the Abbey of Vauclair, dusk had already fallen. There was a torch burning in the bracket on the gatehouse wall. The gatekeeper was arguing with a tinker who was insisting he had business with the royal household. When the man had finally wandered off into the gathering gloom, with his pack weighing heavy on his back, and his dog yapping at his legs, Tom and Alan rode forward.

'Open up, gatekeeper,' said Alan in French.

The gatekeeper eyed them carefully. 'What business do you two youngsters have here?'

'We have been sent to join the King's household. We have a letter of introduction from the Earl of Warwick,' replied Alan, and Tom leant forward and handed a letter to the gatekeeper.

The gatekeeper took the sheet of parchment and examined it. If he had known it was a page from one of the books of the great library of the Abbey of Saint-Vincent at Laon, and what it had cost Tom to write upon it in his best writing, he would have been more impressed than he was. As it happened, he glanced through the letter, but having no Latin, he merely grunted and handed it back to Alan.

'Who are you to report to?' he asked.

'Sir Richard Pembridge, I believe,' replied Alan in that confident way of his.

'You'll find Sir Richard in the hall. Horses to the ostler. Follow the road round to the left.' And with that the gatekeeper withdrew into the gatehouse, and the gates opened to the two boys.

'It can't be as easy as this!' muttered Tom. But it seemed that it was – at least so far.

The two boys saw their horses stabled and then made their way into the kitchens. Tom had never seen so much food in his life. It hung from the ceiling, it lay on the chopping-blocks, it bubbled in cauldrons and it turned on spits in front of the great fire that blazed in the great chimney.

'Where's the smoke going?' gasped Tom.

'Up the chimney,' whispered Alan.

'What's a chimney?'

'It's the latest thing.'

Everywhere, men and women were busy preparing the meal for the King's household. Tom and Alan wandered through and were nodded to or curtsied to for the sake of their smart liveries. They casually took the odd piece of bread and the odd slice of ham and munched them, trying not to look as ravenous as they felt.

'Don't spoil your appetites, young sirs,' said a man in an apron and black hat. 'The King's ordered a great feast to celebrate the meeting-up of the armies.'

'Don't worry, we could eat everything in your kitchen and still be hungry,' Tom felt like saying, but in fact he said: 'We've a letter for the King. Where will we find him?'

The chief cook looked them up and down for a moment and then smiled. Tom went cold inside. 'He can see right through us!' he thought. 'He knows we're no more than a couple of beggar-boys with no more right to be here than a pair of mice!' But the cook nodded towards the kitchen doors.

'You'll find him in the Hall,' he said.

The Great Hall of the Abbey of Vauclair boasted a vaulted ceiling, that soared aloft, aloof and calm. Beneath, all was bustle and hurrying and scurrying. Squires were carrying luggage here and there, others were unpacking. Among the servants strode their masters, in furred gowns and robes with silk linings. Most of them were desperately hunting for the best sleeping quarters they could find. The private rooms had already been commandeered by the great lords, and now the lesser nobles were looking for corners and nooks where they could camp down without too much loss of dignity.

The Chamberlain was rushing here and there telling them they couldn't bed down in that bit of the Great Hall because they'd be in the King's way or suggesting they go and try the refectory or some other part of the building. 'There are just too many of you!' he kept exclaiming. 'I'm going to have to throw some of you out! Only one servant each! D'you hear?'

Suddenly Tom gripped Alan's arm. 'There he is!' He hissed. 'The King!' He was staring at a tall man, wearing a short coat trimmed with white fur flecked with black. He had an arm round one of the noblemen and was

246

whispering in his ear. Tom felt a rush of power to his head: here he was actually witnessing the King of England imparting a state secret to one of the great lords of the realm. The next minute the great lord of the realm gave an almighty bellow, clutched his sides and doubled up with laughter.

'I bet that was a rude joke,' whispered Alan. It had never occurred to Tom that kings might like to tell jokes – let alone rude ones. The King was now smiling happily at the victim of his mirth. The moment looked as good as any.

Alan grinned at Tom. 'Sure you're game for this?'

Tom grinned back. 'May as well be hung for a sheep as a lamb.' He spoke with much more confidence than he felt.

'OK,' muttered Alan. 'Let's go for it.' But as he stepped forward another noble lord caught the King by the elbow and steered him away into a corner.

'Damn!' said Tom.

'Do you really think the letter's going to work?' asked Alan.

'We'll just have to see,' replied Tom. 'Quick! Catch him now!' The King had just broken away from the nobleman and was now frowning. Everyone seemed to be keeping their distance from him.

'Here goes!' muttered Alan, and he stepped forward and knelt in the King's path. 'Your Majesty!' Alan spoke in French. 'I have a letter from my lord, the Earl of Warwick.' And he offered the letter up. A titter of laughter rippled round the room.

The King looked down at Alan. 'You want the King?' he growled. Tom, who was trying to follow the conversation, thought this was such an odd thing for the King to say that he must have misunderstood the French. But the next minute the King turned and called out, 'Father!' and Tom knew why everyone was either laughing or smirking behind their hands: he and Alan had mistaken the Black Prince for King Edward III of England.

At this point, the entire court seemed to fall back, revealing a small, mean-faced man sitting not on a throne but on a small folding chair. The King of England did not look in a very receptive mood. Tom's heart sank. All at once their whole plan seemed so childish – so pathetic. How could he and Alan possibly persuade these sophisticated courtiers that they were anything other than a couple of beggar-boys trying their luck?

But it was too late to go back now. Alan was being pushed towards the King, who scowled at him. An amused whisper swept around the room.

Tom suddenly knew his writing would look ridiculous – so utterly unlike the elegant hand of a court scribe or a learned monk. He remembered trying to think up the right phrases for a great Earl introducing a young relative to a King and he suddenly knew – with total certainty – that this whole plan would look as foolish as it probably was.

But Alan was already on his knee before the King of England. And the King of England had already taken the pathetic letter from his hand. The King of England opened the parchment and ran his eye over it. Then he handed it to a monk who was standing nearby. The monk read it and then bent down and whispered a translation from the Latin into the King's ear.

The King nodded. 'So the Earl of Warwick recommends you to my service?'

'If we can be of use, Your Majesty,' Alan answered, clearly and confidently.

'And where is your companion?'

Tom stepped forward and knelt beside his friend.

'So . . . so . . . two of you,' said the King.

'There really isn't room to take on anybody else, Your Majesty,' said the Chancellor. 'There isn't nearly enough accommodation as it . . .' But the King had silenced him with a wave.

The King shook his head, and Tom was almost certain that the ghost of a smile had crept into those features that looked as if they had not smiled for many years. The King held Tom's letter up by one corner.

'And perhaps you can tell me,' said the King, 'why the Earl of Warwick, for whom I have the highest regard, let me say, neglected to do me the simple courtesy of attaching his seal to this letter?'

Of course! Tom knew there was something missing! Without a seal any letter was obviously a forgery. How could he have been so stupid as to think they could get away with it?

'My lord craves Your Majesty's indulgence,' – Alan seemed quite unperturbed – 'but his seal had been stolen the night before and he was in haste to send us on our way.'

The ghost of the smile seemed to flutter from the King's lips up into his eyes.

'Of course,' he said. 'And probably the same thief stole the Earl's writing paper and forced him to tear a page from a book, in order to write to his sovereign?'

'Exactly, Your Majesty.' Tom couldn't believe Alan could keep up sounding so confident. Their whole plot had been unravelled in the length of time it had taken to read the letter.

'But one thing I find hard to understand.' The King was courteous to an unnerving degree. 'Why should the Earl, who speaks little Latin, as I recall, have bothered to have his letter put into that language, when he knows I prefer to correspond in French?'

That was, Tom had to agree, a pretty big question. Even Alan was taking a few moments to come up with a convincing reply.

But the King hadn't finished: 'However,' he actually smiled at this point, 'the most mysterious thing is why the Earl of Warwick bothered to write to me at all, when he is standing over there.' The King indicated a tall man who was hiding a smile behind his hand.

At that moment, however, one of the nobles stepped forward and bowed. 'Your Majesty,' he said. It was the Duke of Lancaster. 'I am reliably informed that these two young scoundrels are wearing the livery of Sir Galahad de Ribemont, a French nobleman, loyal to King John and the Dauphin. One of my officers is on good terms with Sir Galahad.'

Suddenly strong arms had pinned the boys' arms to their sides. It was all over.

'So young for spies,' murmured the King, as Tom and Alan were hustled off. A ripple of scornful laughter went around the court.

But the Duke had raised his hand. 'Your Majesty! I may have some use for them.'

The King shrugged. 'You may drown them or marry them to your daughters, for all I care, Henry,' he said.

'But, Your Majesty!' exclaimed the Chamberlain. 'Every inch of the place is filled up – we simply haven't room . . .'

But the King had turned away and was suddenly deep in conversation with a woman who had appeared at his elbow.

enry, Duke of Lancaster had established his quarters in the guest house. He had appropriated seven rooms – two for his personal use, one as an office, one as a store-cum-armoury and three for his servants. The Chamberlain had been secretly apoplectic about his taking up so much space, but had not dared say anything to the face of the King's most trusted counsellor.

Tom could not imagine what sort of 'use' one of the most important men in England could have for a couple of young spies. He just hoped it wasn't as door-mats.

One of the Duke's squires had sat them in front of a plate of food in the great man's quarters and was now asking them questions about where they'd come from. Alan was describing their narrow escape from the jaws of a lion and then their hair-raising capture by Genoese pirates off the coast of Africa, when the Duke of Lancaster himself appeared.

He stared at the pair of them for some time, and they kept silent as they ate. Eventually he pulled up a stool and sat opposite them.

His squire gave him a quick summary of everything Alan had told him. Then the great man leant forward and said: 'Now . . . which of you is the Latin scholar?'

'It's Harry,' said Alan, pointing at Tom.

'My name's Tom,' said Tom, ignoring Alan's glare.

'Well, Tom,' said the Duke of Lancaster. 'Why don't you tell me the *real* story?'

When Tom had finished, Henry of Lancaster nodded. Then he stood up and walked across the room, and looked out of the window – even though there wasn't much to see out of it, since it was night and the shutters were closed.

Then he suddenly turned and threw a small scroll into Tom's lap. 'Read it,' he said.

Tom opened the scroll. 'It's a letter! From the Archbishop of Canterbury to the Pope!' exclaimed Tom. 'To His Most Holy and Beloved. . .'

'Yes, yes – skip all that!' said the Duke.

'He asks that he and his servants be absolved from sending any tax for the present year on account of the war . . .'

'That's enough!' snapped Lancaster. 'Very well, Thomas, it would suit me to have someone who is not a churchman to translate these things for me. Would you like to work for me, Thomas?'

'As long as Alan can too,' replied Tom.

'My name's Alan,' explained Alan hastily, 'not Richard.'

'I've no use for a lying rogue,' replied the Duke of Lancaster.

'But he could translate into French for you!' exclaimed Tom.

Henry of Lancaster smiled. Then he clapped his hands

and two large equerries appeared. 'Scrub these two rascals down. They smell to high heaven! Then give them some clothes.' And with that he was gone, and Tom and Alan suddenly realized they were now in the service of one of the most powerful barons in England . . .

But the feeling of elation was to last only a few moments. It was to be overshadowed by an event that was to eclipse almost everything that had gone before.

The two equerries had, by this time marched them to the abbey bath-house, and were now in the process of pulling their clothes off them. Tom, who had never actually sat in a tub full of hot water before, was feeling slightly nervous as he watched the steam rise from the tub, when suddenly Alan screamed.

It was so unexpected that for a moment Tom didn't know what was going on. One moment the only sound was the huff of bellows as a skivvy blew on the fire beneath the tub, the next moment Alan had gone berserk – hitting out at one of the equerries. The other equerry tried to catch hold of him, but Alan kicked and punched him. Then the first grabbed Alan's arms and pushed him down on to the floor, but somehow Alan seemed to have acquired super-human strength. He rolled to one side, kicked at his assailants and was gone.

The two equerries charged after him, and Tom, who was only wearing his breeches by this time, followed. He reached the courtyard in time to see Alan racing across the abbey grounds, pursued by the two equerries. Before Tom had a chance to throw his shirt back on, a number of other servants had joined in the fun. The next minute they had cornered Alan up against the abbey wall.

'The Duke wants him to have a bath!' grinned one of the equerries, 'and he refuses!'

'Get away from me!' yelled Alan.

Tom was now struggling back into his shoes. The small crowd that had gathered round Alan was joking and laughing. There were shouts of: 'Give him a bath to remember!' 'Put him in head first!' and then suddenly several men charged at him, but Alan was too quick for them and in an instant he had shinned up the vertical face of the abbey wall and had disappeared over the other side.

'Alan always was good at walls,' thought Tom.

The men were too surprised to follow.

'What was all that about?' Tom had caught up with one of the equerries. 'What did you do to him?'

'Your friend can't take a joke,' said the equerry. 'Look what he did!' and he removed his hand to show a line of blood across his face.

'Where are you going?' asked the other equerry.

But Tom had already gone. He too had climbed the Abbey wall and was now running after his friend – running into the Forest of Vauclair.

47

'Alan! What on earth are you playing at? We've just landed ourselves a plum position and you go and throw it all away! The Duke'll think we're crazy! What's the matter with you?' These were all things Tom wanted to scream at Alan, as he ran through the forest, but all he actually kept shouting was: 'Are you all right? Alan! Are you all right?'

The winter moon hung above the bare-knuckled trees and filled the forest with ghosts. Alan had run in the opposite direction from the encamped armies, and surprisingly soon Tom found himself swallowed up in a terrible loneliness.

'Alan!' he called. But nothing stirred. Moonlight stripped the bark off the trees and left them like giants' bones sticking up from the ground. 'Alan!'

Suddenly Tom heard a twig snap. He span round and saw Alan's head disappear behind a tree. 'Alan!'

The moon had tried to touch this corner of the forest's heart but had failed. The cold, hard wood kept its secrets in darkness here . . . except that Tom could now hear Alan's breathing close by. 'Alan!' he whispered.

Then he saw him – only he wasn't where Tom had thought he had heard his breath. Alan was standing a little way off, on the other side of a glade that the moon had painted silver for the night. 'Alan!' said Tom, and he stepped forward into the clearing.

Something in the way Alan looked at him made Tom check his step. Something in the way that Alan's eyes turned on him, like a hunted animal's, choked the words in Tom's throat and stopped him asking all the questions he had wanted to ask a few moments before. 'Alan?' he said.

Alan stood there, panting, like a cornered fox who has nowhere else to run. 'I couldn't go on,' he said, and he seemed changed beyond all imagination.

'What happened?' asked Tom. He wanted to rush up to his friend and shake his shoulders to jiggle all the bits of him back into their usual order and remake him into the Alan that Tom knew and loved. At the same time, Tom wanted to hold his friend in his arms and protect him – though from what or why he had absolutely no idea. 'What happened?' he repeated.

'I couldn't go on any more . . .' said Alan.

'You couldn't go on doing *what*?' Tom took a step forward, but Alan stopped him with another look. In the paleness of the moonlight, his face seemed to radiate an energy that Tom could not understand at all. Alan seemed at one and the same time to be exhausted, hurt, defiant and fearful. 'What couldn't you go on doing?' asked Tom.

And then, as far as Tom was concerned, the most extraordinary thing that had happened, or that was ever to happen in the whole of his adventures, happened. Alan pulled off first his shirt and then his breeches, and then stood alone in that silver glade, naked in a pool of moonlight, and he was a girl.

'Pretending,' said Alan. 'I couldn't go on pretending.'

· 48 ·

Tom would have been speechless if he'd had the time, but a hand had already grabbed him round the throat in a grip like a man-trap. And a voice that he recognized with a feeling of hot dread growled in his ear: 'So – now I've got the full set!' The next moment he was spun round and staring into the face of the Priest.

Alan had already pulled on her clothes and bolted into the undergrowth, before two dark shapes sprinted across the glade after her.

Tom felt the point of a knife pricking his neck. 'Now, now, boyo, nice and easy-like. Wouldn't want no accidents happening, would we now?' growled the voice.

There was the sound of a struggle in the undergrowth beyond the glade, and the Priest's two henchmen returned with Alan.

As the two youngsters were bundled through the forest, Tom couldn't catch Alan's eye. He couldn't speak. He couldn't even think. Everything had happened too quickly.

'Well, isn't this cosy!' said the Priest. He had just pushed them into a clearing where a fire was burning. In the far corner of the makeshift camp, tied to a tree, was the crumpled, unhappy figure of Sir John Hawkley.

'What a touching reunion!' The Priest was clearly very pleased with himself.

As Tom and Alan were trussed up with great speed, Tom couldn't help being impressed. 'They're obviously experts,' he thought to himself. 'I bet they've tied up more people, prior to torturing and killing them, than I've eaten hot chickens! Look at this! I can't move a muscle! I can't move my feet or my hands . . . I can just wiggle my fingers a bit, but . . .'

'Stop wiggling your fingers!' growled the man with the cauliflower nose, who was tying him up.

'So you thought you'd left us to fry in that hell-hole, did you?' The Priest had marched over to the miserable Sir John, whose face was bruised and whose nose had a trickle of blood oozing from one nostril. 'Well, does this feel like I'm dead?' The Priest suddenly struck Sir John violently across the face; his head snapped back and the blood sprang out of his nose and down on to his jerkin.

Tom looked across at Alan . . . 'Alan'? He didn't even know what to call his friend any more. She was white and breathing hard, but when she looked across at Tom, he realized that although everything had changed, nothing had changed. There was still that defiant gleam in Alan's eyes, still that bold look that took on the whole world and dared it to do its worst – still the hint of mischief. Tom – inexplicably – felt a surge of relief. Alan was still Alan.

But the relief lasted for an instant so brief that it hardly happened. The Priest had grabbed Alan's face in one hand and was squeezing it so that she looked like one of those gargoyles that poked out from under the Abbey roof. 'Where is it? Eh? We know he got some silver like – so what we want to know is what's he done with it?'

260

Sir John raised his head and tried to speak, but his mouth was full of blood and several teeth were missing. In fact, judging by the way coherent speech eluded him, Tom assumed his jaw had been broken. But there was little doubt he was warning them not to say anything.

'Ask him,' replied Alan nodding towards Sir John. 'I don't know what he's done with it – and neither does Harry.' Alan added this last bit hurriedly as the Priest turned on Tom.

'What's he done with it, Harry?' The Priest was using the tone of voice a fox might use to ask a chicken if it minded being eaten uncooked.

'My name's Tom.' Tom didn't have the first clue why he should be trying to keep the record straight at a moment like this. Alan rolled her eyes.

The Priest looked from one to the other. It was as if he were weighing something up in his mind – which is, in fact, exactly what he was doing. 'Which one is the canary, d'you reckon, boys?'

The man with the cauliflower face smirked and pointed at Alan. 'He'll sing.' Tom breathed a sigh of relief. Somehow or other these villains had not seen what had passed in the glade.

'Agreed,' said the Priest, 'but he's a crafty one . . . we can't trust him. No sir. Whereas this little sprat . . .' and he lifted Tom up by his ear and then dropped him.

'Ow!' said Tom, as the Priest walked over to Alan. 'Leave my brother alone!'

The Priest turned. 'Wait! Wait! Don't tell us everything at once, little one,' he said. 'There's plenty of time.'

Sir John growled something inarticulate. Alan stayed silent and watched as the Priest pulled a stick out of the fire. He put the flame out and then blew on the end of the stick until it glowed red. Then he waved it in front of Alan's face.

'Such fine soft skin, look you now,' whispered the Priest. 'It'd be a shame to mark such a complexion I'm thinking,' and he held the glowing point dangerously close to Alan's cheek. Alan tried not to flinch.

Tom struggled to free himself, but knew it was hopeless. Sir John spat out a sentence of unrecognizable words.

'Now, you little heathen, I'll baptize'ee with fire, that I will,' the Priest was grinning into Alan's face, 'unless you tell me the truth. Where is the silver?'

'I'll tell you!' Tom found himself talking. 'Leave him alone! I'll tell you everything you want to know!'

Sir John gave a yellful of blood and teeth.

The Priest didn't look at Tom. He kept staring at Alan and moving the glowing point ever closer to her cheek.

'He hid it in the Abbey wall!' shouted Tom before he knew what he was saying. 'Forty paces to the left of the main door, there's a loose brick. It's behind that!'

The Priest still didn't look round. He still held the red-hot ember up to Alan's face, grinning with malevolence. Alan finally flinched and moved her head back. As if he'd got the reaction he wanted, and could now turn his attention elsewhere, the Priest span round and looked at Tom. Then he glanced across at his men. 'Well, boys, what d'you think?'

The man with the cauliflower nose grunted. The man with the cauliflower ear nodded, and the man with the cauliflower face spat out the words: 'Could be.'

'Could be indeed,' grinned the Priest. 'I think this little sprat warbles the truth.'

'Of course it's true!' exclaimed Tom with convincing indignation.

'It better be true,' replied the Priest. 'I forgot to tell you: if it isn't true, when I get back, I'll kill you – from the outside in.' Tom didn't quite understand the threat but he still felt sick in his stomach.

'Dog and Gilly, you stay with these three,' the Priest went on. 'John Dover and Break-skull come with me!' and he had thrown down the red-hot brand and was on his way.

Tom had never felt so alone in his life. He felt he might have made a big mistake, but he couldn't ask Alan for advice. He couldn't ask anybody. He was all alone, and he couldn't see a way out: the Priest would go to the wall; he'd find Tom had been lying, and he'd come back and kill him – from the *outside in* – whatever that meant!

Tom wanted to scream at Sir John: 'For God's sake tell them where you've hidden the stuff! It doesn't matter about a bit of silver! It's our lives that matter!' But he knew he couldn't even do that without giving the game away.

All was not well, however, with the Priest's henchmen. The two who had been told to stay behind with the prisoners had been whispering hurriedly together. Now one of them called out: 'Wait!'

The Priest stopped and turned. 'What?' he growled.

The man with the cauliflower face looked uncomfortable. 'We're coming with you,' he managed to say.

'You're staying to guard the prisoners!' growled the Priest.

The man with the cauliflower face struggled to say: 'Supposing it's true and the silver's in the wall – how do we know you'll come back with it?'

Tom could see the man's problem; he wouldn't have liked to voice such dark suspicions to the Priest's face either. The Priest snarled back: 'What are you saying, Dog?'

'I'm only saying,' replied the man named Dog, 'what's to stop you three running off with the silver and splitting it among yourselves? In any case, how do we know you'll bring it *all* back. You might just bring a bit of it and save the rest for yourselves.'

'Yeah?' This was the only contribution to the debate that the man with the cauliflower ear was to make, and yet it seemed to clinch it. The Priest glanced irritably at the other two. Then he looked at their prisoners.

'All right. Those three aren't going anywhere anyway,' he muttered. 'Come along of us if you must.' And without more ado the five of them set off.

As soon as they had disappeared, Alan and Tom burst into a frenzy of inactivity; that is to say; they struggled to loosen their bonds but found themselves trussed so tight they couldn't move. After a few minutes they both realized it was useless. As for Sir John, he seemed to have lost consciousness – or hope – and was slumped against the tree he was tied to in a crumpled heap. Alan looked across at Tom. 'My name's Ann,' she said.

'My name's Tom,' said Tom. 'It's nice to meet you properly at last. A bit late for striking up a long friendship, but there you go.' Tom didn't understand why he felt so bitter.

'I'm sorry,' said Ann.

'So,' said Tom, avoiding her gaze, 'the Priest'll come back and kill me, and then I suppose he'll kill . . . What are we going to do, Alan?'

'Ann . . . I'd like you to call me by my name . . .'

'We're going to die, Ann. It doesn't matter what we call each other!' Tom was close to tears, but they were tears of anger. He was angry that he was going to die so soon. He was angry that he was going to die so young. He was angry that he couldn't do anything about it. And he was angry that he had been deceived by his friend.

'I always knew I couldn't believe anything you told me,' he said. 'But . . . How could you? All those things you said about girls and . . . You were lying to me! Every day! All the time!'

'I'm sorry, Tom.' Ann spoke quietly and quickly. 'I had to. Anyway, it's true what I said about girls not being allowed on expeditions like this. I couldn't have done any of the things I have done if people had known I was a girl. Sir John would never have taken me on for a start.'

'I feel like an idiot!' Tom could hardly listen to what Ann was saying.

'I'm like you, Tom,' she said, and urgency had crept into her voice. 'I'm a runaway too. My father wanted to marry me off to this old man. It was 'for the good of the family', he said. I *had* to run away! But how could I run away as a girl? I wouldn't have got past the gates!' She looked at Tom, and a tear trickled down her cheek. 'I didn't mean to deceive you. Forgive me, Tom.'

'They're coming back!' Tom could hear angry voices approaching through the forest.

'Tom!' said Ann. 'I want you to know I love you, little Tom! I'm sorry it's ending like this!'

But Tom didn't really hear her. He had suddenly noticed a small wooden object lying on the ground.

· 49 ·

The small object on the forest floor was something he'd forgotten all about – and yet it had been hanging round his neck through all his adventures. It was only during the rough handling he'd received from the Priest's men that its thong had snapped, and the thing had fallen out of his jerkin.

It wasn't much of an object to look at. It was made out of plain wood and it was old and worn, but Tom knew in a flash it might just be their salvation.

'The Wolf Whistle!' he murmured, and he rolled himself over to it.

In the forest he could now hear the Priest's voice cursing and snapping at the others as they got closer and closer.

Tom manoeuvred himself so that his lips could touch the whistle. The next moment he'd got his mouth around it and he'd rolled over on to his back.

'What on earth are you playing at?' Ann's voice was twisted up with tension, as the undergrowth crunched beneath the feet of the Priest's men.

'The Wolfman told me to blow it if ever I need the help of the wolves!' Tom wanted to explain but there was no time. The Priest's angry face had already appeared from the darkness of the trees, lit up by the

266

camp-fire like the Devil's face in Hell.

Tom blew. He blew with all his might and with all his soul on that little wooden whistle, that had become his last faint hope of survival in this world. He blew, knowing it was his last chance. But as he blew, his life with the Wolfman and the wolves in the Great Wood seemed so far away and so unreal that it was like someone else's story in another book. Suddenly a wave of despair crashed over him and sent his mind tumbling. It seemed ridiculous that he could have believed that he had ever talked to wolves, or that he could expect this crude wooden whistle to summon the help of any living creature in this far-away forest.

But still he blew it and blew it, and now he felt himself truly drowning in the sea of despair, for no matter how hard he blew he couldn't produce any noise whatsoever – not a single peep. The whistle didn't even work! He spat it out in disgust, just at the same moment that the Priest burst into the the clearing.

'So the boyo's a liar after all!' There was almost a note of triumph in the man's voice – as if he were glad that someone who he thought would tell the truth had proved to be no better than himself. Or perhaps it was glee in the anticipation of the pain he now felt free to inflict upon Tom, that put a spring into his step. 'Who'd have thought it?' he smiled. 'Such an innocent-looking lad . . .' and he grabbed Tom's hair and pulled him roughly across the clearing.

The others had arrived by this time. The man with the cauliflower ear had started kicking Sir John. 'What's up with the old fool?' he grumbled.

'He must be Gilly,' thought Tom. And then he

thought: 'Why am I thinking about stupid things like who's called what, at a time like this?'

The Priest, meanwhile, had decided to give Gilly a hand, or rather a foot, for he was now also kicking Sir John. 'Come on, you drunken sot! Wake up! D'you hear?'

Sir John groaned, and tried to open one eye. The Priest grabbed his head and twisted it round so he was staring right into Tom's face. 'You see this young lad? Eh? D'you see him?' Sir John managed a weak groan. 'Look at him, damn you!' screamed the Priest. 'And listen! I'm going to start cutting bits off him, and I'm not stopping until you tells me what you've done with that silver!'

Sir John tried to say something but only managed a slurred drool. If Tom's heart could have sunk any further it would have done, for he realized that even if Sir John were to tell the honest truth about what he had done with the silver, nobody would be able to understand him.

The Priest, meanwhile, had produced a knife. 'Now where shall we begin, boys?'

The henchmen chuckled nervously. 'Take his ear,' said John Dover – the man with the cauliflower nose.

'Toes first!' said Dog – the cauliflower face. 'Allus start with the toes.'

But Ann had struggled herself into a sitting position. 'Stop it!' she screamed at them. 'Leave Tom alone! You're animals! Leave him alone!'

'Well well . . . seems like you care for this little scab more than your master does. Very well. *You* tell me where the stuff's hidden.'

'I don't know!' yelled Ann. 'We told you – Sir John ran off with it – we haven't seen him since!'

'Then I'll just take one of this little fellow's fingers . . .'

said the Priest, and he rolled Tom on to his stomach and pulled one of his fingers so it stuck up free of the bindings. 'And when I've taken this finger, if you still can't tell me, I'll take another and then another until you *can*!'

Tom shut his eyes. He couldn't believe this was happening to him. And yet the pain as the Priest pulled his finger seemed to disappear as an avalanche of images suddenly crashed through Tom's mind: the view from Hound Tor, the Wolfman's hut, the city wall they'd climbed, the night-watchman, the burning inn, the port of Sandwich on fire, the shipwreck, the friar, the siege of Laon . . . Each image was as bright and as clear as anything he'd ever seen with his actual eyes . . .

And then two things happened. First of all he felt the cold steel of the Priest's knife touching the middle joint of his finger. Secondly he heard a voice in his head say: 'What do you want? You called for help!'

For a moment Tom couldn't think what was going on. And then he suddenly he found his mind replying of its own accord: 'But the whistle didn't work!'

'It sounds a note only wolves can hear,' said another voice.

Tom kicked and twisted round to look for the wolves who were talking to him. He did this at the very moment that the Priest brought his blade slashing down at Tom's finger, with the result that the Priest missed his mark and gashed his own finger instead. 'Ow!' he cried. 'You little . . .'

But Tom didn't hear any more. He might not be able to see a wolf anywhere, but his head was buzzing: 'Tell us what you want!' cried several more voices.

'You see these men who have captured us and wish to harm us?' he found his mind saying. 'Help us!'

But the Priest, his hand covered in his own blood, had grabbed Tom's finger again and raised the knife. 'You little rat!' he snarled.

'No!' shouted Ann.

The next second there was a howl – as if all the wolves in the world had suddenly howled at once.

'Look out!' screamed the man with the cauliflower face, and the Priest turned to see a sight he had hoped never in his life to see: thirty or forty timber wolves were leaping from the undergrowth, and bounding across the clearing towards him, jaws snapping and teeth bared.

The Priest dropped the knife and ran – he didn't even have time to think of screaming. The others followed suit, and in a matter of seconds, the camp was cleared.

The fire had been scattered in the mêlée, and the burning charcoals lit up the forest floor with a hundred red points of lights. Sir John's bloody mouth was hanging open, the odd broken tooth showing in the dimness. Ann looked across at Tom with confusion written more clearly across her face than relief. But Tom had no time to explain. He turned to the lone grey wolf that had hung behind.

'There is one thing more,' he said, although not aloud. The wolf sidled up to him, as if uncertain who he was, and Tom turned to show the wolf his tightly bound hands. 'Set me free,' he whispered and the wolf started to gnaw at his bonds.

In a few minutes Tom was free, and before the howls of the chasing wolves and the screams and curses of the Priest's gang had disappeared over the horizon of sound, he had freed both his companions.

· 50 ·

'Nothing may be what it seems. Everything is not necessarily what you expect.' Tom was muttering this to himself as he rode at the back of the Duke of Lancaster's retinue. 'If Katie could see me now, she'd think my dream had come true. I'm a squire to one of the greatest lords in the land, and I'm on my way to battle. But it's not like I imagined, Katie, not one bit of it! I don't even know if it's what I want any more!'

The rain was pouring down on the King of England's army as it made its miserable way towards the great city of Reims. It was there that Edward was to be crowned King of France – or at least that was the plan.

The current King of France was a prisoner in England, captured in battle by the Black Prince three years ago. His throne was being filled in his absence by his sickly, timid, eighteen-year-old son until his people could raise the vast ransom demanded by the English. In the meantime, the whole realm of France had fallen into chaos.

Powerful nobles vied with each other to wrest the throne from the young prince, while in Paris the townspeople had revolted against the king's taxes. And all this was being played out against a desolate landscape that had been burned and wasted by the English over the last twenty years.

Edward of England, however, seemed to be of the opinion that, in these circumstances, the people of France would welcome anybody strong enough to impose some sort of order on their country, and – as far as he could see – he was just the man! He was ruthless, a good organizer, well versed in court intrigue and political manoeuvring, a good dancer, charming with the ladies and, into the bargain, he'd more than thirty years' practical experience of ruling a factious country. On top of all this, he just happened to be the French King's cousin. He was the perfect man for the job, even if he said it himself.

So it was that Edward had assembled the grandest army ever to leave England, and was now marching to Reims, whose citizens, he hoped, would welcome him with open arms and crown him King of France.

That was the theory. But nothing may be as it seems. For a start the King and his planners had not reckoned on this rain. Even military strategists plan their campaigns for bright sunny days. Nobody plans to do anything in the rain – certainly not in rain like this: rain that got into the baggage, rain that got into the stores, rain that got into the back of your neck, rain that even seemed to get into your skin.

Tom looked around at 'the grandest army ever to leave England': banners hung limp and clammy, the colours running; plumes on helmets drooped in rats' tails; the bright coat-armour, surcoats and horse trappings were all the colour of mud, because that's exactly what most of them were covered in. The very soldiers themselves seemed little more than bags full of water in which their bones were floating around loose, as they slopped about on their saddles, or sloshed behind on foot.

Since their escape from the Priest, neither Tom nor Ann had seen much of Sir John Hawkley. The great man hadn't thanked them nor even told them where he was going; he had simply grabbed the nearest horse and ridden off as fast as its legs could carry him.

The Duke of Lancaster had received the two friends back with some amusement. 'So, the maid didn't want to take a bath at the hands of my equerries?' he smiled. Ann didn't reply. 'The sooner we get you into skirts, "Ann", the sooner we'll stop making mistakes like that,' said the Duke.

But Ann looked him straight in the eyes and replied: 'My Lord, I have served as a squire for the last two years, and no one has ever questioned my abilities. I wish to carry on in that capacity. I do not want to wear skirts.'

A ripple of protest went round the room. The Duke of Lancaster laughed out loud. 'A female squire!'

'It's impossible!' said the Chamberlain.

'It's ridiculous!' said the Steward.

'It's not fair!' cried the other squires.

But the Duke laughed out loud again. 'You're a bold one, young lady!' he said. 'What is your family? Where do you come from? For I never yet employed a squire without knowing who his father was.'

'Except me,' thought Tom.

'My father wished me to marry a man I could neither love nor respect, my lord,' Ann replied. 'That is why I ran away. I would willingly tell you my father's name, but only if you guarantee me your protection.'

'Young lady,' said the Duke, 'I cannot take the side of a daughter against her father.'

'Then I cannot tell his name.'

'Then you cannot be of my company,' replied the Duke.

Ann bowed and turned on her heel and began to walk out of the chamber. Before she reached the door, however, the Duke called out: 'Wait, young lady.'

Ann turned and looked directly at the Duke.

'You are a wilful child, and I thoroughly disapprove of what you have done. Your father has every right to say who you should marry if it is in the interests of his family. It is an act of disobedience and disrespect to have run away,' said the Duke.

Ann stood alone, her head held high, her gaze on the Duke unbroken.

'I am sorry to have offended both my father and your lordship,' she said, and turned to go again. But the Duke called her back once more.

'It is also an act of courage,' said the Duke, 'and though I may not approve of the act, I approve of the spirit behind it. I wish all the young men who now serve under me as squires had half as much pluck.'

Ann did not move.

'You shall join my retinue . . . as a squire.'

A shock wave went around the room, followed by loud protests, particularly from the Chamberlain, but Henry of Lancaster silenced everyone with his hand, and turned his mind to more important affairs of state.

It was still raining as King Edward's great army finally reached its destination. The twin towers of the great

Cathedral could be seen reaching up towards the gloomy sky. The city walls glistened with water running down the stonework. And Tom stared at the closed gates and the fortified towers and wondered what he would tell his sister about all this.

He had come so far, and yet now he was here he felt he had not arrived anywhere. The dreams he had whispered to Katie, as they lay in the hay at home, were still no more than dreams. The Court of Prester John and Kublai Khan, the deserts of Arabia and the land of Saladin, the plains of Asia, the glittering streets of Constantinople and the frozen wastes of Russia – they all seemed as far away as ever. The here and now seemed strangely ordinary, even though this too had been part of his dream.

'It's an odd thing,' Tom whispered to Ann, as they lay talking together in the Duke of Lancaster's rooms that night, 'but the things I'd always dreamt about doing are not nearly as exciting as the things I'd never imagined.'

'You're talking in riddles, Tom,' replied Ann.

'Am I?' said Tom. And he laughed. He laughed as he remembered the village priest going off to sell his dog, and how he'd irritated the holy man by falling in the pond.

'It's all going to happen! Just like I said it would,' exclaimed Tom.

'What?' said Ann who was nearly asleep.

'But the only thing is: now I know what not to expect!' Tom was still laughing.

'What don't you expect?' yawned Ann.

'The most exciting things that happen to me! That's the whole point!' cried Tom. And suddenly he gave a great yell: 'Saladin!' And stood on his head.

'Tom!' whispered Ann. 'Whatever are you doing?
'I'm starting to be myself!' Tom replied.

The next morning the siege of Reims began.

THE END OF THE FIRST ADVENTURE

Choosing a brilliant book
can be a tricky business...
but not any more

www.puffin.co.uk

The best selection of books at your fingertips

So get clicking!

Searching the site is easy – you'll find what you're looking for at the click of a mouse, from great authors to brilliant books and more!

Read more in Puffin

For complete information about books available from Puffin – and Penguin – and how to order them, contact us at the appropriate address below. Please note that for copyright reasons the selection of books varies from country to country.

www.puffin.co.uk

In the United Kingdom: Please write to Dept EP, Penguin Books Ltd,
Bath Road, Harmondsworth, West Drayton, Middlesex UB7 ODA

In the United States: Please write to Penguin Putnam Inc., P.O. Box 12289,
Dept B, Newark, New Jersey 07101–5289 or call 1–800–788–6262

In Canada: Please write to Penguin Books Canada Ltd,
10 Alcorn Avenue, Suite 300, Toronto, Ontario M4V 3B2

In Australia: Please write to Penguin Books Australia Ltd,
P.O. Box 257, Ringwood, Victoria 3134

In New Zealand: Please write to Penguin Books (NZ) Ltd,
Private Bag 102902, North Shore Mail Centre, Auckland 10

In India: Please write to Penguin Books India Pvt Ltd,
11 Panscheel Shopping Centre, Panscheel Park, New Delhi 110 017

In the Netherlands: Please write to Penguin Books Netherlands bv,
Postbus 3507, NL–1001 AH Amsterdam

In Germany: Please write to Penguin Books Deutschland GmbH,
Metzlerstrasse 26, 60594 Frankfurt am Main

In Spain: Please write to Penguin Books S. A., Bravo Murillo 19,
1° B, 28015 Madrid

In Italy: Please write to Penguin Italia s.r.l.,
Via Felice Casati 20, I–20124 Milano

In France: Please write to Penguin France S. A.,
17 rue Lejeune, F–31000 Toulouse

In Japan: Please write to Penguin Books Japan, Ishikiribashi Building,
2–5–4, Suido, Bunkyo-ku, Tokyo 112

In South Africa: Please write to Longman Penguin Southern Africa (Pty) Ltd,
Private Bag X08, Bertsham 2013